TRACK DOWN IRAQ

A Brad Jacobs Thriller

Book 4

SCOTT CONRAD

PUBLISHED BY:
Scott Conrad

2nd Edition © June 2018

Copyright © 2017 - 2019
All rights reserved.

No part of this publication may be copied, reproduced in any format, by any means, electronic or otherwise, without prior consent from the copyright owner and publisher of this book.

A Brad Jacobs Thriller Series by Scott Conrad:

TRACK DOWN AFRICA – BOOK 1

TRACK DOWN ALASKA – BOOK 2

TRACK DOWN AMAZON – BOOK 3

TRACK DOWN IRAQ – BOOK 4

TRACK DOWN BORNEO – BOOK 5

TRACK DOWN EL SALVADOR – BOOK 6

TRACK DOWN WYOMING – BOOK 7

Visit the author at: ScottConradBooks.com

I come in peace, I didn't bring artillery. But I am pleading with you with tears in my eyes: If you fuck with me, I'll kill you all.

Marine General James Mattis, to Iraqi tribal leaders, 2003.

Table of Contents

PROLOGUE

He prayed that his death would be quick and violent instead of slow and painful. The black-robed DAESH troops were particularly brutal towards the mercenaries when they captured them. He had seen the brutality firsthand, and it was not pretty.

Brandon Murphy, or "Murph", as he was known by his friends, squatted in a dark corner in an alleyway in the Al-Tameem neighborhood of Mosul, Iraq. As he fought to catch his breath, he wiped the dust from his face with the tail of his ragged, black-and-white checkered kaffiyeh. The kaffiyeh was de rigueur for locals, and it concealed Murph's decidedly European features from the militants as well as from the Shia militiamen supporting the Iraqi troops.

Murph and five other Belus security contractors were the only members left of the support team

Belus had committed to Iraq's Golden Division, elite U.S. Special Forces trained Special Operations troops of the Iraqi Army.

Belus was a huge private military company with close ties to the Iraqi government and had been hired by the State Department as "advisors" to Iraqi Special Ops. Murph and a platoon of Belus security contractors had been embedded with the Golden Division just prior to the November 1 dawn commencement of Operation "We Are Coming, Nineveh." Within hours of the onset of hostilities, all pretense of Murph's status as trainer and adviser had been abandoned, and the platoon was spread over the entire division in groups of six.

Special Operations leaders detailed them to problem areas, where Murph and his companions resolved particularly thorny situations enabling their Iraqi counterparts to continue with their missions. By the third day they operated mostly independently, though they received instructions via radio. By the time they reached the Al-Tameem neighborhood of Mosul, they were so far separated from the Golden Division troops that they were having trouble getting resupplied.

They had long since been forced to replenish their ammunition, ordnance and other supplies from the bodies of DAESH insurgents. They accepted what food and water they could get from citizens who refused to abandon their homes because of the fighting. Batteries for their radios were not available, and the one Murph carried he'd resorted to turning on for only moments at a time. The battery was so close to dead he had no idea if his transmissions were getting out; he sure as hell wasn't getting much in the way of radio traffic.

He no longer knew if any friendlies knew where the hell they were or even if anybody cared. He was also having a hell of a time telling who was friendly and who was not. Even the Golden Division troops were not all in a common uniform.

Many of the players in this damned war looked pretty much the same, and the Iraqi regulars had abandoned so much equipment when Mosul fell in June of 2014 that they were driving Humvees and carrying M-16s and CAR-4s.

A burst of automatic weapons fire erupted at the end of the alley. The sporadic sounds of gunfire had become so commonplace that the sound itself did not startle Murph. But when the bullets began to slam into the concrete block walls around them, sending shards of concrete and a great deal of cement dust into the air, the mercs scattered and returned fire. In seconds the action was over, the shooters having moved on without Murph and his companions never having caught a glimpse of them.

Murph was no stranger to combat. A former Force Recon Marine, he had seen action before, most notably in 2004 in the second battle of Fallujah. When he left the Corps, he became a "security contractor", which had become the politically correct term for "mercenary". His decision to leave the Corps had nothing to do with his patriotism; it had more to do with financial security.

As a mercenary, he still fought against his country's enemies and for their allies, but the difference in pay was staggering to the point of ridiculousness. As a contractor, he was paid almost twenty times what he had made as a Marine. At the moment, he was questioning whether he had made a poor decision despite his fat bank account. The Corps would never have abandoned him the way Belus seemed to have. Marines didn't leave their comrades behind.

He wrapped the tail of his kaffiyeh around his face to keep from breathing in the concrete dust and checked to see if anyone in his tiny group had been hit.

"Count off!" he barked. It was force of habit more than anything else. He could see all five men, but it did serve to let him know none of them had been hit. They counted off one by one and he gave the hand signal to move out. He needed to find a deserted home or business, one they could easily defend while they caught their breath. The men needed rest, regardless of their dire circumstances. Murph had long ago learned that rest was a weapon, just as much as the rifle in his hand.

They followed him like ducks in a row, about fifteen meters apart. It wasn't necessary to tell them how far apart to space themselves. The men were experienced. In open terrain they would spread out further, in close quarters they would move closer together... It was team S.O.P. (Standing Operating Procedure).

Murph led them out of the alley and along the outer edge of the rubble strewn, unpaved main street, watching all the time for movement on the street or the rooftops along it. After they moved quietly for several blocks encountering no other people, insurgents or civilians, he looked for an obviously abandoned building.

In short order he found one with thick mud brick walls and a minimal number of openings for windows and doors. Standing in the open doorway, Murph waved the others inside. Taking one last look up and down the street, he decided they had not been seen, so he ducked inside.

The five mercs stood in a semicircle, their eyes on him as he removed his kaffiyeh and reached for his canteen.

"Unass your gear, guys. I'm pretty sure we weren't spotted coming in here, so we should be okay for a short while. Hydrate as best you can, grab a little chow, and rack out for a short-short. I want one man on lookout at all times, we rotate every hour.

"You're up for the first watch, Thompson." He pointed at the most experienced of his little band as he spoke. Thompson had served with him in Force Recon, and the veteran moved immediately to secure a vantage point from which he could observe the street in both directions. The others, professionals all, began to field strip and clean their weapons before eating or sleeping.

Murph stripped down his M4A1, wiping the dust and grit from its surfaces with a tack cloth, reapplying a few drops of lubricant before reassembling it. The process, which he could have done in his sleep, took only a few minutes. When the weapon was back together, he turned his attention to his personal weapon, the one he had brought from home, a Glock 17 with an extended magazine. Over his years of experience, he had come to trust the weapon for its reliability and the availability of ammunition no matter where he was in the world. Murph knew that accuracy and placement were far more important in combat than "knock down power".

His weapons tended to, Murph reached inside the thigh pocket of his camouflage fatigues and removed a brown paper wrapped packet of pache. The Mosul favorite was a piece of animal intestine stuffed with rice and a veritable witch's brew of animal (usually lamb) parts that would be thrown out as scraps anywhere else on Earth. The inhabitants of Mosul, however, loved the stuff. When begging for food, Murph found that it was best not to be too finicky.

Despite the gross ingredients, pache didn't taste too bad, and it did provide nourishment and energy. Still chewing the cold pache, Murph moved from man to man, checking their ammunition status and mental state, chuckling and joking to take some of their tension away. It was only after he had sat with Thompson for a few minutes that he returned to his spot near the door and sat cross-legged on the floor.

Murph slipped off his kaffiyeh and pulled a half heat tab from another pocket and set it on the concrete floor. He used his scarred old Kabar knife to make a kind of stove from a discarded can and placed the heat tab inside. From another pocket he took a folded half packet of MRE ration coffee and poured it into his canteen cup, to which he added water. Lighting the heat tab, he set the cup atop his field expedient stove and began to stir the beverage with a plastic spoon, which he kept in the breast pocket of his fatigues. He'd held on to the spoon because he had no idea when he'd get another one. They had been unable to get supplies from the allies for more than five days.

He added a pinch of cardamom, a gift from a grateful Iraqi civilian, to the nasty tasting instant coffee. The people of Mosul dearly loved their coffee, adding cardamom for flavor, and Murph had acquired the taste, though DAESH had all but shut down the industry when they had taken the city. They used as their rationale the fact that women had to raise their niqab (veil) and expose their faces to drink it and because they called the clinking sound the coffee vendors made with their small china cups to notify prospective customers of their presence haram, which translated as "dance of the devil."

Murph finished the coffee and had another pache from his packet then leaned back against the wall and closed his eyes. There was so much running through his mind he felt certain he would not be able to rest. Thirty seconds later, he was fast asleep.

The blast from the grenade woke him up. In his sleep he slipped down the wall he was leaning against and ended up prone on the floor, face down. His position had spared him. Groggy and befuddled from the concussion, Murph struggled to sit up. Even in his confusion he could see that the other four men in the room were quite obviously dead. He knew his lookout had been neutralized or killed; else the grenade would never have been tossed into their sanctuary.

He was still shaking his head, trying to clear it, when the black-hooded militants rushed into the room, roughly shoving him back against the bare concrete wall and relieving him of his weapons. Murph had studied Arabic at the Defense Foreign Language Institute at Monterey, California, so he understood what the bastards were saying. He was still alert enough to keep all expression off his face as he listened to them so they wouldn't know he could understand them.

One militant pointed his M-16 at Murph's head and Murph watched as his finger started to squeeze the trigger. Time seemed to freeze as he watched the brown finger ease back on the trigger. Instead of seeing his life replaying itself as he had always thought he would, Murph simply felt cold and alone. Almost as if he was dreaming, he heard the leader order the militant to lower his weapon.

"Do not shoot him, Khalif. Perhaps we can find a use for him."

The militant lowered his weapon, muttering something that Murph didn't quite catch, and then lifted the rifle high, bringing the butt down hard on Murph's chin. Everything went black.

*   *   *

He recovered consciousness slowly, having no idea where he was. His hands were bound behind him, and he lay face down on a hard surface that smelled like concrete. Sand flies continued buzzing around his face, attracted by the dried blood. He felt a dull pain in his left calf, but he forced himself to perform a thorough check for injuries without alerting his captors to the fact that he was conscious.

His tongue probed in his mouth, finding that two of his teeth had been knocked out and three more were loose, undoubtedly from the butt stroke administered by the hooded jihadist. A careful self-inspection revealed a few sore spots, but nothing serious ... until he reached the ache in his calf. Evidently a bullet or a piece of shrapnel had struck him there. His fatigue trousers were stiff, sticky, and stuck to his skin, so apparently the bleeding had stopped.

Satisfied that he wasn't in imminent danger of dying, he silently prayed that his death would be quick and violent instead of slow and painful. He had seen the brutality of the black robed DAESH troops firsthand, and they were particularly brutal towards the mercenaries when they captured them. The only real hope he had was if the leader thought he could be traded for something or someone they wanted. When his prayer was finished, he slowly opened his eyes.

A lone black ant scurried about beneath his face, its antennae probing. Across the otherwise empty room, a sand spider crawled along the base of a rough concrete block wall. There was a steel door, and there were no windows at all. He sat up and began to work his wrists, trying to get out of the restraints.

ONE

"You ain't right, Ving," Willona Ving said with a laugh. Nathaniel and Jordan, their two sons, were laughing as well. Ving sat at the table, a massive platter of bacon in front of him. He and Willona had prepared breakfast for dinner, with Mason Ving handling the chore of frying the bacon because Willona never fried enough to suit him, even though his passion for what he called "baconating" was well known to anyone who knew him.

Willona had made biscuits, scrambled eggs and a pot of grits, and cut up some fruit. The boys set the table as Ving hummed happily over the griddle.

A retired forty-seven-year-old Force Recon gunnery sergeant, Ving was a massive black man, six feet tall and two hundred and sixty pounds of muscle, tendon, and bone. He had acquired a small pot belly since his retirement from the Corps, but it hadn't slowed him down at all. His skin was so black it had blue highlights in the light of day, and his bald head shone in any kind of light. His smiling brown eyes could turn deadly and reptilian when he was pissed, and his friends had learned over time that when his eyes went flat, it was best to be anywhere else.

It was not as if the man couldn't be friendly; he had a deep, warm voice that wasn't at all what one would expect to hear coming from the mouth of a Force Recon gunnery sergeant. He sounded very much like the actor James Earl Jones. When he did get riled, that same voice could sound as if it was coming from the lungs of Satan himself, but that was not a common occurrence. His sheer bulk and his attitude were intimidating enough to be sufficient to cover most circumstances, even in the heat of battle, but with Willona and the kids he was a gentle bear of a man.

Willona dished out helpings of everything and buttered her homemade buttermilk biscuits, while

Ving deposited a generous portion of bacon on each of the others' plates before dragging the platter over in front of his own. It wasn't as if he wouldn't give more out if the boys asked for it, but he pretended to grump about it when he did.

"Daddy, may I have some more?" little Jordan asked, holding his plate towards his father.

"Boy, you gonna turn into a piece of bacon if you don't watch out," Ving remarked with a fierce scowl as he lifted several rashers of the crispy meat and settled them on the boy's plate. Both boys giggled and Jordan held his own plate forward wordlessly. Ving forked over another generous portion and tried unsuccessfully to conceal his smile from his wife.

It was true that he really loved bacon, but only Willona knew how and why that passion had developed. Ving had been raised in a rented shotgun house in a bad part of New Orleans, and his family had been dirt poor. As a child, he had

18

watched his poor momma, old before her time from taking in laundry as well as working at anything that came her way to help support Ving and his brothers. She had died when Ving was twelve, but every day of her life she had fried fatback, which was all they could afford, for breakfast every morning.

There had barely been enough of the cheap fatback to go around, and once Momma had passed on to Glory, Ving had noticed that his daddy often pretended not to want any so that the boys could have his share. As much as he loved the taste, Ving decided that at twelve he had become a man, and he emulated his father, giving his share of the delicious smelling fatback to his brothers, who were both smaller built than he was. He joined the Marine Corps as soon as he was able, so that his daddy wouldn't have to work so hard to support him and his brothers.

His first morning in the Corps had been a revelation. He'd been confused and a little worried about all those guys in uniform screaming and yelling at him. And more than once he'd considered decking one of them for calling him a sonofabitch before he'd realized that they weren't really calling his beloved momma a bitch, it was just a cuss word.

His attitude changed once he'd been herded into the chow hall with the rest of the boots. He held up his compartment tray and they loaded him down with chow—and, miracle of miracles, they had put real bacon on it. Nice, crispy bacon that crunched when you bit into it and tasted like Heaven on Earth. After that first breakfast, nothing on Earth could have chased him out of the Corps.

He always sent money home, but while his buddies in the Corps spent their pay on drinking whiskey and chasing women, he spent his in little mom and pop restaurants getting his fill of real bacon, which, to his delight, tasted far superior to fatback. The craving for bacon had never left him.

The four of them ate and laughed, enjoying the warmth and companionship of a truly close family, sharing the events of their day. As they talked and joked, Ving kept a half eye on the television in the living room, which, as usual at this time of day, was tuned to the national news. Willona didn't really approve of the distraction, mainly because the media tended to upset her husband when they deviated from just reporting the news to slanting it to fit their own agenda, which, of late, seemed fairly often.

Nevertheless, she didn't object. Mason Ving was a man of many interests, and he knew things because of his close association with Brad Jacobs and his career that ordinary citizens simply weren't aware of. Ving kept up with the happenings in the world, even though Willona would have preferred that he stop working and enjoy his retirement. That was a fruitless hope. She realized that Ving needed the action and the adrenaline. If he quit he would become an old man in no time at all, and that was something she knew she could never ask him to do.

Jordan had just made a teasing remark about his father's "baconating" when Ving's head jerked sharply towards the television set. He set his fork down and put his big hands on the table, a partial mouthful of his bacon unchewed. He didn't respond to Jordan's remark, his attention was riveted on the television. After a moment, he finished chewing his bacon, wiped his mouth with a napkin, and then left the table, his supper unfinished.

Willona heard him turn the volume up on the TV and then heard the sound of him changing channels with the remote as he sought something. She sensed something was wrong, but she also knew better than to ask him about it. When he was ready, he would tell her. Instead, she hushed the boys and hurried them through their supper.

After they were finished, she sent them to their room to do their homework while she hurriedly cleared up the dishes and washed them. She placed the leftover biscuits on the unfinished platter of bacon and covered the whole with a clean cotton dish towel, knowing Ving might want to snack on it later.

When she had finished in the kitchen, she dried her hands and went upstairs to check on the boys. When she felt satisfied that they were completely engrossed in doing their homework, she walked back downstairs and sat in her recliner, watching the broadcast Ving was so intent on. Ving remained totally immersed, rigidly focused on the reporter on the screen. The word "Mosul" flashed on the TV screen, as well as the reporter's name, and then a montage of images and film clips raced across the screen.

The reporter paused and then started another segment from the same location. He started talking about one of the big military contractors, a company called Belus. He explained a little about the company's history, observing that the company had originally been called Marduk Services LLC, a name which struck a familiar chord in Willona's consciousness. It was a name she had heard fairly often when Ving and Brad had talked over beer and barbeque.

Many of their friends worked as "security consultants" for various firms. Most of the security companies maintained solid reputations, but Marduk Services LLC had not been one of them. She remembered the night the company had been sold because Brad and Ving had argued over whether the new owner, Parker Willingham, would be any different than the original owner.

Several of the men who occasionally worked for Brad had called him on his cell phone that evening asking him for his opinion, and Brad had refused to endorse Willingham because he had never worked with him before. He explained that he had no negative information about the man to the callers, but Ving hadn't agreed.

They had both heard rumors, but Brad refused to repeat them because he had no firsthand knowledge. Ving had heard the rumors from people he knew and trusted, but they were not men Brad knew. Ving had taken offense at Brad's reluctance, but Brad's personal code wouldn't permit him to repeat the rumors.

Willona remembered being irked at what she felt was a slight to her husband. But Ving had explained to her later that night that Brad's integrity and unwillingness to violate his personal beliefs was one of the main things he admired most about his friend.

"Brad is a rock, baby," he had told her. "He don't bend, and he would never turn his back on a friend.

I've been to Hell and back with him and I know."
He had hugged her tight, kissing her softly as his
hands roamed her nightgown clad body, exciting
her as he always did. She'd shivered as his massive
hands found her breasts beneath her nightgown,
teasing her and taking her mind off the topic of
conversation. But she'd never forgotten.

She'd remembered the conversation as she'd
walked back downstairs and taken a seat on the
sofa, watching her husband as he opened his
laptop and picked up his cell phone. Curiosity was
killing her, but she wisely kept her silence,
focusing instead on listening to Ving and trying to
read the emotions on his face, which was easy
enough most of the time but virtually impossible
when he was "in the zone". It remained a side of
her husband she didn't much care for, but it was a
side that made him the consummate professional
he was, and it had always brought him home
safely. For that reason, she never tried to change it.

"Brad, it's me, Ving. Call me the instant you get this message, it's urgent." He hung up the phone with an expression of frustration on his face.

"Damn it! What the hell is he doing that's so important he won't answer his phone?"

Willona spoke up.

"You used to be a bit more of a romantic, big fella," she said softly, allowing her hands to rest on his neck, her fingers automatically kneading the muscled flesh. His muscles were tensed and hard, and she wanted to soothe him. "Surely you didn't forget that he picked up Vicky at the airport this afternoon."

*   *   *

Vicky Chance, the lithe and seductive redheaded Immigration and Customs Enforcement agent, had joined them at the Mexican resort the team had used as a jumping-off point for their Amazon mission. Her association with them had begun after she figured out what they were up to during a very intense physical liaison with Brad Jacobs that had turned from a flirtation into something more. The man they were after, Rodolfo Abimael Guzmán, was heavily involved in human trafficking and Vicky had been chasing the elusive bastard for a couple of years.

There had been a "Black Warrant", which was a euphemistic term for termination order, on Guzmán issued by the C.I.A. after their "Wet Work" specialists had failed to take him out. The bounty on his head was rumored to be in excess of a million dollars. Neither Vicky nor Brad was interested in the bounty, but they agreed to join forces and combine their resources in the hopes of sneaking the man back into Texas and turning him over to the government for prosecution.

That plan had gone awry when Jessica Paul, Brad's beautiful treasure-hunting cousin, had freaked out after seeing firsthand the victims of Guzmán's child snatching ring. Guzmán, injured in the firefight to free Delroy Ving and the children, had crawled towards an escape door in the makeshift prison he was holding Delroy and the kids in. Jessica had caught him, and in a fit of cold rage, had stuffed a thermite grenade down the front of his expensive hand tailored Lord & Taylor safari pants and pulled the pin.

Guzmán did not survive the encounter. Brad refused to claim the bounty. He shed no tears over the man's death, but he refused to accept the mantle of "killer for hire".

Vicky had taken a round high in the chest when everything had gone to hell, but it was a through and through that had done relatively minor damage. When the team eventually returned to Cabo San Lucas, she had spent a week recuperating at the Hacienda Beach Club … in Brad's bed. The two had been inseparable, but to the team's astonishment, Vicky had left at the end of the week. All Brad would say about her leaving was that she needed a little time to think. All of them had been pleased when Brad announced that she was coming to join the team more or less permanently.

*   *   *

The television screen blinked and suddenly there was film of a man kneeling in the dirt, a black garbed terrorist holding a wicked looking blade at the man's throat. A reporter was doing a voiceover, explaining what was happening. There was no mention of the man's name, but it was clear from the Velcro U.S. flag patch on his shoulder that he was an American. Ving's lips pulled into an angry grimace.

"Shit!" Ving muttered as he reached for his cell phone again. Willona knew not to interrupt, so she focused on the news story. A talking head from the U.S. State Department came on-screen, reminding the reporters present that, as a matter of policy, the U.S. government does not negotiate with terrorists.

"Do we know the name of the prisoner?" one of the crowd of reporters asked.

"All I can tell you at this time is that we are aware of the man's identity and that he is not currently a member of the U.S. Armed Forces. We will release his name as soon as we verify that his family has been notified."

"Idiot!" Ving fumed. "You just let the whole world see his face! If his family didn't already know it they do now!" The spokesman had done nothing to alter Ving's opinion of the State Department, which he considered by and large as staffed by over-educated incompetents who lived insular lives in ivory palaces that existed only in the minds of liberals.

He reached for his cell phone again and angrily punched the speed dial number for Brad's cell phone. When he reached Brad's voice mail again, his massive index finger stabbed at the "end call" button, and then he set the phone back down.

He glanced over at Willona.

"I need to go get Brad."

*   *   *

Willona had been around the block a few times, and she understood a thing or two about mission prep. There was no question in her mind that the man being held by the jihadists was someone her husband knew and knew well. The set look on his face was his "mission face", and that meant, come hell or high water, Ving was about to leave again.

It always frightened her when he left on one of Brad's missions, and it had always scared her when he did it on active duty. Her man seemed to think he was invincible, but she knew every inch of him, had cataloged every scar ... she knew better. She also realized there were a ton of things he needed to do at the moment that he could do without Brad.

She was being a little selfish, which she admitted to herself. Vicky Chance was a good-looking woman of child bearing age. She was also savvy enough, sexy enough, and mean enough to keep Brad Jacobs occupied forever. Willona was not about to let Ving interrupt that budding romance over an hour or two head start. It appeared clear that neither Ving nor Brad was ever going to give up their profession.

She wouldn't ever pressure Ving to give it up anyway; he would not be the same man if he didn't do what he was born to do. But if Vicky could keep Brad preoccupied with that gorgeous figure of hers, maybe Ving would spend less time away and more time with his family. There was certainly enough money for Ving to retire, her investments and her buying and selling had built up a comfortable bank account that would see the boys through college and with enough left over to see them both through their old age.

Ving had been surprised that she had been able to front the money for the Amazon mission. He had no idea just exactly how much she had accumulated over the years; if he had known, he would have been shocked. That money hadn't even made a small dent in her portfolio.

*   *   *

"You will do no such thing, Mason Ving! Brad will contact you as soon as he gets your voice mail." She reached over and grabbed his laptop, setting it down on the coffee table before him.

"Here, get started gathering your intel. I'll go start a fresh pot of coffee, and by the time Brad gets here, y'all should be ready for the rest of that bacon and some biscuits." She bent forward and kissed him tenderly.

TWO

Brad Jacobs and Vicky Chance were not watching the news. Vicky, a tall, lithe woman with dark red hair, incredibly long legs and high, firm breasts, had luminous jade-green eyes with improbably long lashes. Her lush mouth curved into a smile that promised everything, and at the moment, it was doing so in a way Brad found incredible. The two of them were engaged in some very serious foreplay that was getting more intense by the moment, while romantic music played softly over the speakers in Brad's apartment.

Brad's cell phone rang and he groaned and fumbled for the device, but Vicky chose that exact moment to try something no woman had ever been able to do before. The sensation was so overpowering that he uttered a low moan and let the phone fall from his fingers to the floor. The fingers of his other hand clutched convulsively at the sheets and the hand that had dropped the cell phone went to the back of her head. Vicky's low chuckle was muffled, and Brad forgot all about the phone. A moment later, Vicky raised her head.

"Who was that?"

Brad groaned and pressed her head back down.

"Doesn't matter," he gasped. "I have voice mail … and if it's really important they'll call back…"

Vicky chuckled again, much clearer this time, and returned her attention to her task. A few minutes later, the phone rang again, and this time she crawled off the bed and went to collect the annoying gadget from the floor. By the time she had reached it, the ringing had stopped again. Lifting it up, she glanced down at the caller ID on the display and handed it to Brad.

"You're going to want to take this." She waved it at him so that he could see the display. "It was Ving." She handed him the cell phone and then reached for her robe, which was draped across the bedroom chair. Brad held the phone in his hand, his finger poised over the speed dial key assigned to Ving's number as he watched hungrily as Vicky covered her bare frame with the robe.

"Whatever the hell he wants, he's got horrible timing," Brad muttered as he pushed the key. Ving had to be sitting with his phone in hand because he answered before Brad heard the first tone sound on his own.

"Brad?" Ving answered.

"Yeah buddy, your timing really sucks!"

Ving was not amused. "Have you seen the news tonight?"

"Hell no, Ving, I just picked up Vicky at the airport a couple of hours ago. Why would I be watching the news?"

"Bad tidings, brother. It's Murph, and he's in deep shit. It's all over the news channels."

"Jesus, what happened to Murph? Last I heard he was working as a shooter for Belus." (Shooter is an industry term for security contractor hired to take an active role in military or paramilitary activities rather than as a trainer or advisor.) Brad sat up in the bed and reached for a pen and steno pad.

"He stepped in it big time, Brad, got himself captured by them DAESH bastards. It's on all the news channels. Hell, they even showed him sittin' on the ground with his hands cuffed. The bad guys are braggin' that his ransom will arm a whole battalion of jihadists. You need to check it out... I've already started the research."

"Research?"

"Don't tell me you ain't plannin' on goin' after him, Brad... I've known you too long. Besides, you know as well as I do that the U.S. has a standin' policy that says we don't negotiate with terrorists and we don't pay ransom." When Ving grew pissed, his normal vocabulary reverted back to the one he had in the old days when he was just another boot, straight off the block in New Orleans.

Brad grunted in agreement.

"Okay Ving, give me an hour to catch the news and then call Jared. It's going to be a long night."

"Roger that, Brad." The connection went dead.

He didn't even bother to get dressed. Naked and carrying the steno pad and pen, Brad padded into the living room and sat down in front of the big screen television. Picking up the remote, he turned the TV on and immediately changed to the twenty-four-hour news channel. The story on-screen was concerning some plane crash in Oklahoma City. Brad split the screen and started sifting through other news channels for the story Ving had told him about.

*   *   *

Vicky watched her lover, a little in awe of his intensity as well as a little miffed at his ability to put her out of his mind while her body was still in a state of extreme arousal. Still, she heard the concern in his voice when he asked Ving about their friend, and she was more than a little knowledgeable about Belus and their current situation in Iraq.

She had left the military intelligence field and signed on with I.C.E. to concentrate on human trafficking, particularly sex trafficking involving minors. It was I.C.E.'s reticence to get involved in cases of that particular abomination in allied countries that had made Brad's offer of a place on his team so attractive.

She was dying to know what kind of trouble their friend was in, and she became more than just curious about who "Murph" was. She understood Brad well enough by now to realize that the best way to find out what she wanted to know was to listen. Tying her sash around her robe, she walked out into the kitchen to start a pot of coffee and set out chips, sandwich meat, cheese, and bread for snacks. If Ving and Smoot were coming, it was going to be a long and hungry night.

One of the screens flashed to the story Brad was looking for, and he quickly isolated it and turned the sound up. The reporter was speaking off camera as a video played on-screen. Vicky returned to sit on the far end of the sofa so she wouldn't distract Brad. She needn't have worried, Brad's entire being was focused on the television.

On-screen stood a group of black clad jihadists, their faces covered and most of them holding black banners with Arabic words. The "Black Banner" is a traditional flag of Islam dating back to Muhammed himself. The variation used by the Islamic State of Iraq and the Levant (DAESH) represents the second phrase of the shahada in the form of a representation of what is allegedly the original seal of Muhammad.

The white circle signifies the seal, bearing the three words Allāh Rasūl Muhammad, "Muhammad is the prophet of Allah." The wording is a variant of the second part of the conventional form of the shahada, "Muhammad Rasūl Allāh." DAESH is essentially an Arabic acronym comprised of the first letters of the group's original name in Arabic, "al-Dawla al-Islamiya fil Iraq wa al-Sham." The acronym has no meaning in Arabic.

DAESH also sounds very much like an Arabic verb that translates to "tread underfoot, trample down or crush something." The word is unpleasant sounding to Arabs and the group's proponents take violent exception to its use; the leadership has gone so far as to issue an edict ordering that anyone who uses the derogatory term is to have their tongue cut out.

All the jihadists appeared heavily armed, many with M-16s, others with AK-47s. The spokesman for the group cradled his weapon in his arms, while the others carried theirs slung over their shoulders. At his feet knelt a battered prisoner, his face bloody and dirty, wearing the desert fatigues very similar to those currently worn by U.S. Army forces in the region. Brad muttered an imprecation when the camera focused on the prisoner, and Vicky heard him exclaim, "Murph!" under his breath. Beat up as he was, apparently he was still recognizable.

Off camera, the reporter was saying that the leader kept accusing the prisoner of being a spy of the U.S. and demanding an incredible ransom of twenty million dollars U.S. and the release of a dozen prisoners at Guantanamo Base in exchange for his repatriation. Otherwise, he would be beheaded in a public place in two weeks' time. Brad snorted derisively at the demand.

"As if! They know damned well we don't negotiate with terrorists!" His fists were bunched up, his knuckles white from the strain.

Vicky raised one eyebrow inquisitively, but Brad was fixated on the TV screen and didn't notice. Her patience at an end, she chose a more direct method of inquiry.

"Who is this guy, Brad? A friend?"

Brad didn't look away from the screen.

"His name is Brandon Murphy, baby, and he's more than a friend, he's a brother."

Vicky waited patiently for him to explain further.

"Murph damned near got himself killed in Fallujah back in 2004 saving two injured Marines during Operation Phantom Fury, two guys everyone else had given up for dead after they had stupidly stumbled into an ambush on a recon patrol. The guys were both hit bad, and Murph, rather than wait for reinforcements, made his way through some really withering fire from a crew served weapon and a squad of riflemen to the two Marines and held off the bad guys until help arrived, which was nearly six hours later.

"It was bad, really bad. At times it got down to hand-to-hand. The last time the three were hit before the reinforcements arrived, one of the two original guys was out cold, nearly bled out. The other two held off the jihadists with knives and fists. All three had to be medevaced out by chopper."

His voice choked up, and he seemed to be having trouble getting it under control. Vicky, sensing there was more, kept her mouth shut but reached across to lay her hand on top of his comfortingly. He finally got his voice back.

"I woke up in Landstuhl (Landstuhl Regional Medical Center in Kaiserslautern, Germany) plugged into a ventilator and with more tubes coming out of me than I could count." He turned to face Vicky. "When I passed out, I didn't expect to ever wake up, and I believed Ving was dead. The last thing I remember seeing before everything went black was Murph struggling with one of those camel jockeys, one hand around the guy's throat, the other hand jamming that Arkansas Toothpick of his up under the guy's ribcage. He was snarling like a mad pit bull and bleeding so badly his uniform was soaked."

He was staring at the screen again, where Murph was being roughly handled by the jihadists. Vicky watched as he struggled to his feet in a rage and then winced as one of the men in black administered a textbook buttstroke to his chin with an AK-47.

"Sonofabitch!" Brad cursed.

She understood Brad's emotions at that moment, certainly better than any civilian on Earth could have. She recognized the debt Brad felt to this

"Murph" guy. She had been saved more times than she cared to admit by a comrade-in-arms.

She could still clearly remember the last time, when a skinny Army PFC had suddenly appeared from around a pile of concrete rubble in a Kandahar back alley and killed a jihadist who was trying his best to take her head off with a wickedly sharp curved khukri. The vivid memory still had the ability to send a shudder through her svelte body.

Brad turned to her.

"You realize I'm going to get him, right?"

She nodded.

"This is personal, baby, you don't have to come on this one. I owe this guy my life."

Vicky stood up and wrapped her arms around him tightly.

"From now on, Brad, I go where you go. That's the only way this is going to work." Vicky knew her strengths and limitations. As far as she was concerned, women like Willona were the ones who suffered the most, waiting at home to find out if their men were alive or dead. When it came down to guts, the Willonas of the world were the real heroes.

She cradled his head between her small, firm breasts for as long as he would allow her to, but he soon turned back to the TV screen, scribbling notes on his steno pad, his face a mask of concentration. She noted with relief and satisfaction that he hadn't argued with her when she said she was going with him. She headed for the bedroom to shower and change before Ving and Smoot showed up.

"You know," she said over her shoulder as she left, "you should probably give Charlie a call. I'd bet a dollar against a donut that his State Department and C.I.A. contacts are going to know a hell of a lot more about this than the news media."

Brad didn't even glance at her as he reached for his cell phone.

THREE

Brad speed dialed Charlie Dawkins' cell phone and waited impatiently for him to answer. Charlie had recently been "separated" from the U.S. Department of State's little known enforcement arm. He hadn't come right out and admitted it, but Brad suspected that Charlie's involvement in the team's recent activities in the Amazon had a lot to do with the separation.

Charlie proved himself in both Alaska and the Amazon, and Brad felt no qualms about adding him to the team. Charlie had worked for the Department of State as a Federal law enforcement agent when Brad first met him in Alaska. He had been Jessica's boyfriend at the time, she had told Brad that the man reminded her of her favorite movie character, Indiana Jones. Charlie even looked a little like Harrison Ford, the movie actor who played the character.

Brad's relationship had been tenuous with Charlie at first, but Charlie had eventually confessed his true purpose in coming along with Jess on the trip. He also managed to gain the team's respect. His affection for Jessica Paul turned out to be genuine.

"Dawkins." The brusque answer was a little surprising since Charlie was generally a pretty easy-going guy. The explanation for Charlie's atypical answer was cleared up a second later when Brad heard the unmistakable sound of his cousin Jessica's voice, giggling in the background. He realized he should have expected that, Charlie and Jessica seemed to be joined at the hip these days.

"Charlie, it's me, Brad. I hate to interrupt whatever I'm interrupting, but the shit has hit the fan and I need you. How long would it take for you and Jess to get over here?"

Brad had no intention of letting Jessica go along on this mission; he was still feeling guilt over her taking a bullet in the thigh down in Peru. He did not, however, want to get into a pissing match with her over the phone, so he invited her as well. It didn't occur to him until hours later to wonder why he was so against Jess coming along but had not even considered not taking Vicky.

Charlie assured him that the two would be at his apartment within the hour, and then he hung up.

*   *   *

Vicky returned from the bedroom barefoot, wearing one of Brad's chambray work shirts with only one button fastened between her breasts and a pair of cutoff denim shorts that looked as if they had been sprayed on. A conservative outfit for the sexy exhibitionist. She pulled her dark red hair back into a ponytail, which she draped over her right shoulder, letting it hang down over the pink scar tissue left by the bullet wound she had suffered in Peru. She sat down on the sofa close enough to see what Brad was looking at on his laptop and scribbling on his steno pad, but not close enough to distract him.

It was only about fifteen minutes later that the front door opened and Ving trooped into the living room, followed closely by Jared Smoot, the lanky Texan, and Pete Sabrowski, the only other man on the team that was as big as Ving. Brad was so focused on his research he didn't even look up to greet them, he just called out to them over his shoulder.

Jared and Pete were former Recon Marines, men who had served with Brad and Ving both separately and together. Jared was a highly decorated sniper, probably the most skilled man with a Barrett .50 caliber sniper rifle that Brad had ever seen, and he had seen the best the Corps and the Army had to offer. Pete was a pilot who could fly just about anything that would get off the ground, and he was a stone freak with explosives as well as a hell of an operator.

Vicky, flashing Brad an exasperated look, rose gracefully from the sofa and hurried over to hug the men in turn, greeting them with a warm smile and a pleasant word or two. She met Ving first, wrapping her arms around his massive neck and planting a moist kiss on his cheek. He had to bend over for Vicky to hug him, and her arms barely managed to encompass his neck and shoulders.

Jared Smoot was right behind Ving. He was pure Texas cowboy from his close-cropped hair down to his boots and jeans. He held a broad Stetson in his hand as he bent down to accept his hug from Vicky, and he blushed when she kissed his cheek. She would never have known from looking at him that the man was a maestro with a Barrett .50 caliber sniper rifle and a legend within the ranks of Special Operations snipers.

As she hugged him, Vicky remembered that he would drink coffee in a pinch, but he had a penchant for hot cocoa that rivaled Ving's addiction to bacon. He possessed his own special recipe for the hot drink, which he explained to Vicky in great detail during their stay at the Hacienda Beach Club after the Amazon mission. She would have to make some for him.

The last man through the door was Pete Sabrowski, a great bear of a man whose primary function with the team was as a pilot. Vicky was surprised to see him because he had picked up some kind of bug in Peru, probably from the river crossing swims in the Amazon, and been slow to recover. Brad had told her that Pete could fly anything that had a seat big enough to hold him. He maintained a great sense of humor and an affable personality, but Vicky had seen him move in the field. Pilot or not, the man was a proficient shooter, a real warrior.

When she had greeted the men, she waved them towards the kitchen.

"There's food and coffee in the kitchen, guys," she said. Then she winked at Jared. "I haven't made your cocoa yet, but I'm headed that way." Three pairs of eyes watched Vicky's progress towards the kitchen, which in truth, was a breathtaking sight. After a moment, Ving followed her, followed by the others.

Vicky searched through the pantry for the ingredients for Jared's special cocoa and found that she was missing a couple of key components. She turned, and with her brightest smile on her face, held out her hand to Smoot. The big rangy Texan managed to carry what he called his "makin's" wherever he went, and he drank hot cocoa before he settled down to sleep no matter how damned hard it was to prepare it.

Brad had told her he'd watched Jared scoop a hole in the desert floor near Fallujah, within sight of the Taliban troops they were surveilling on a long range reconnaissance patrol. Jared dug deep into the sand behind a shallow dune and made a stove out of a tin can, perforating top and bottom with the tip of his custom knife. He placed a heat tab inside the can then donned his poncho, bent over the makeshift stove so that no light could escape to give him away, and then carefully struck a match from one of his MRE accessory packs. The lanky, raw-boned Texan was mean as a snake in a firefight.

"You don't have to make my cocoa, Miss Vicky," Jared drawled, but he was already reaching for the deerskin drawstring bag that held what he called his "makin's" tied to his hand-tooled leather belt. He would need the energy he got from the sugar to get through the marathon brainstorming session that the night was sure to become. Ving had already explained to him what was going on as they waited for Pete to show up.

*　　*　　*

When Jessica and Charlie arrived, they found Brad and the others sitting around the dining room table, a massive and ancient rustic wooden piece that Willona had discovered on a buying trip to San Antonio. On a whim, she lugged it back home and refinished it herself as a gift for Brad when he got his new apartment. She had left all the old cuts and scars in the surface, a testament to the table's age, and then used a self-leveling polyurethane finish to smooth it out. Brad loved the old table.

Pete was the first one to notice the pair. "Hey! You two come on in and take a load off!" Charlie walked over and sat down immediately while Jessica went straight to Vicky and gave her a hug before slipping into the chair beside her.

The conversation continued unbroken by the interruption.

"What do we know about Belus' efforts to repatriate Murph?" Ving asked.

"I'm not even sure they're doing anything right now," Brad said sourly. "I've been in contact with Ed Rogers from China Post #1 and he hasn't heard a word. He's putting out some feelers and has promised to get back to me as soon as he hears something."

China Post #1 of the American Legion was formed in Shanghai, China in 1919. The post went into exile in 1938 when Japanese forces overran Shanghai before the U.S. officially entered World War II. Communist forces took control of Shanghai in 1948 and confiscated "The American Club," the Post's official location, and its property. The Post operates in exile without an official location and acts as a point of contact for former Special Operations personnel and as a sort of clearing house for jobs and intelligence for what are often referred to as "Soldiers of Fortune" or "mercenaries".

"Belus?" Charlie asked, his mouth forming a moue of distaste. "Used to be Marduk LLC?"

"The very same."

"Is Jack Rainey still heading up that outfit?"

"The last I heard, he's still the owner, but I heard he'd put it up for sale." It was Ving who'd offered that tidbit of information. He had noted the rumors circulating around Marduk and the way its employees were disrespected. His character wouldn't allow him to spread rumors; as he understood it, the only reason the company managed to hire professionals was because in an industry legendary fabled for its high wages, Marduk paid at the top of the scale.

Rainey had been a Marine, though he hadn't been Force Recon. For that reason alone, Brad was reluctant to say anything negative about the man, but his experiences with Marduk LLC had been anything but satisfactory. It was a pillar of his own philosophy that respect and loyalty were things that had to be earned and that they had to work downwards in the chain of command as well as upwards.

Rainey demanded the respect and loyalty of his employees, but he neglected to return it. One brief association on a job in West Africa had convinced Brad that he no longer wished to associate with the company. Since the company had restructured he had avoided any contact, mostly because Rainey remained at the helm.

Charlie chimed in. "Belus is in danger of having their contracts with C.I.A. yanked right now. The State Department has received a rash of complaints from clients and former employees. I don't have any of the specifics…" He shook his head. "I'm not sure that's going to happen though. They've got deep pockets, and they're in bed with some very powerful people on the Hill…"

Charlie had not been forthcoming about the nature of his separation from the State Department's enforcement arm, and none of them had felt like prying. Charlie had earned his spurs in Alaska and then proved himself again on the Amazon mission. It was possible that he told Jessica, but if he did, she had not revealed it to anyone.

"Charlie, can you think of anyone who might have any knowledge regarding this situation specifically?" Vicky asked. "Maybe someone who works in the Middle East Section or someone who has recently come back from there and might have some pertinent information."

Charlie glanced down at his wristwatch and did a few quick mental calculations.

"It's still early in D.C., I might be able to find someone..." He removed his cell phone from his breast pocket.

"You can use my office, Charlie," Brad broke in. "The blue phone is a secure line." The encryption software Brad used was compatible with most secure telephones, a product of a genius pal of his who had been an N.S.A. employee for years before breaking out on his own to found a software company.

As Charlie left the room, everyone took advantage of the hiatus to visit the bathrooms and then graze on the snack offerings Vicky had put out for them.

"I left a whole platter of bacon and biscuits at home!" Ving hollered in a mock-anguished voice.

"There's bacon in the fridge and an electric griddle under the counter, Ving," Vicky said drily. "I'm not *that* domesticated." She turned to Jessica, who was daintily nibbling on a banana. "You need to eat that sideways, dear, lest you overstimulate our poor neglected Neanderthals."

Jessica spluttered and choked before sailing off into gales of laughter.

In a lower voice, Vicky pointed at Jessica's thigh and asked how her recovery was coming.

"Pretty good," Jessica said. "I managed five miles on my run this morning. It's still a little tender, so it slows me down just a hair."

"Strong enough to work if we go on this mission?" Vicky murmured.

Jessica's eyebrows raised inquisitively. "If?"

"Brad feels guilty about both of us getting hit on the last one. I think he's going to try to use that as an excuse to keep either of us from going to the Middle East," Vicky muttered under her breath.

"Oh *HELL* no!" Jessica exclaimed in a loud voice, turning her head to glare at Brad.

"Oh shit!" chuckled Ving. "Incoming!"

"What did I do?" Brad asked, confused.

Ving grabbed his arm and guided him back to the table. "Back to work, brother. I have no doubt all will be explained to you in short order … but you need to watch your six. My sixth sense tells me you're about to get ambushed." The big man was smiling.

"If I was you, Brad," Pete said through a mouthful of pastrami and rye sandwich, "I would be looking for my Kevlar turtle hat and flak vest." He was grinning, and crumbs were tumbling unnoticed from the corner of his mouth.

FOUR

The task of being a diplomat fell to Jared, who was still at the table, sipping at the oversized china mug of his special cocoa.

"By all accounts," he said, "we got us an all-out scrap in full bloom in Mosul right now. From what I could see on the news reports, the 1st Commando Battalion, part of the 1st Special Operations Brigade managed to fight its way into the Gogjali quarter of Mosul. They were the first unit of the Golden Division to enter the city."

Iraqi Special Operations Forces (ISOF), generally known as the Golden Division, is the Iraqi Special Forces unit formed by coalition forces after the 2003 invasion. The Division is run by the Iraqi Counter Terrorism Service and comprises three subordinate brigades. The First Commando Battalion formed the hard tip of the spear of Iraq's finest warriors, though in the team's eyes the group was the equivalent of a regular U.S. infantry battalion.

"Yeah," Brad mused, "but that ain't the only thing that affects a P.O.W. snatch op right now. There are other operations, other units, which could really put a kink in any op we decide to mount."

"Not just in Mosul, either," Ving pointed out. "DAESH in Mosul is actively engaged with U.S. backed forces in Sirte (Libya), Raqqa (Syria), and al-Bab (Syria) as well as being involved in smaller terrorist plots all over the world. Face it, the N.S.A. computers are sifting through every phone call, email, and social media conversation in the country referencing Mosul, DAESH, ISIL, or anything relevant to the subject. Face it, the only thing we've got protecting us is the sheer volume of reports the N.S.A. is filtering."

"Shit," Brad grumbled, slamming the pencil in his hand to the table top in an uncharacteristic display of temper. "Even my Google searches are being monitored."

"Probably," Ving agreed.

"If anyone has thought it through yet," Vicky said thoughtfully, "they've possibly already constructed an algorithm for a search that specifically isolates inquiries by licensed security contractors, Brad. If they have, you can expect at best a phone call from someone in the State Department, and at worst a knock on your door and a visit from a serious guy in a very conservative suit wearing sunglasses."

"Shit!" Brad said again. He stood up abruptly. "I must be losing it," he said, shaking his head. "I'm covered as far as the internet goes. I spent a lot of time, effort, and money setting up multiple Virtual Private Networks. Anyone, even N.S.A., trying to run down my I.P. address is going to be chasing their tail for weeks. Where I haven't been smart enough is using my cell phone."

"I don't think you have to worry about that very much, Brad," Vicky observed. "So far all you've done is contact Ving and Charlie on your cell phone. Even if the existing algorithm N.S.A. is using picks up on any of the keywords you've used, it will take an incredible amount of time for them to go over every message they picked up today and single you out.

"You've got to remember there must be millions of messages trapped every single day. By the time they come up with the algorithm to isolate security contractors several days will have passed and the number of messages they have to filter through will be in the billions."

"I think the lady has a point, Brad," Jared said. "What's said and done is said and done. We all just need to keep in mind that we must keep a lid on our communications from here on out."

Pete snapped his fingers. "Brad! What was that captain's name in the brigade commo section in Kandahar?"

"Captain Dieter?"

"Yeah, Dieter," Pete said happily. "I seem to remember that he got out of the Crotch and started up his own company here in Dallas. Now that I think of it, his company makes apps for cell phones ... security apps. I bet he could help us get our commo secured in a hurry. Does he owe you any favors?"

"I don't think so, but we got along well. It doesn't matter though. There aren't that many of us, I can cover enough cell phones for all of us if we need to change."

"Thought the war chest was runnin' kinda low after bringing Delroy back," Ving said.

"I have a reserve that will keep us for a while, Ving, don't worry about that."

"I'm just sayin', Brad. If you need help on the cell phones, just let me know," Ving grumbled.

Brad made a mental note to get hold of Eric Dieter the next morning as early as possible. "Okay, all open communications within the team except through my secure phone are to cease and desist. If you can't avoid any of the keywords, then don't talk except face-to-face. I'll get our commo squared away in the morning."

He stopped to make sure everyone understood before going on. "Any research you need to do computer-wise needs to be done from here in the apartment, off my server." He glanced over at Ving. "I know I have to be leaving something out, Ving. Have you got anything to add right now?"

Ving rubbed his bald pate with one hand as he scrunched up his face the way he always did when he was concentrating. Before he could speak, Jessica spoke up.

"You've always told me that no mission ever goes as planned, Brad, but you also told me that the biggest reason missions go bad is because of lousy or poorly misunderstood intelligence. I understand that this is personal, and that Murphy is not only a brother but a brother you feel indebted to, but you guys"—she glanced briefly at Brad and Ving individually—"need to come to grips with the fact that the only thing we can do right away for Murphy is to accumulate and assimilate all the intelligence you can before we go wheels up on this mission."

At the words "we go wheels up," Brad opened his mouth to object, but Jessica cut him off at the knees.

"Don't even start with me, Brad. I'm healed, my thigh is fine. I did five miles in thirty minutes this morning … and I'm coming with you. I'm a member of this team now, and I have the right!" Her pretty jaw jutted forward aggressively and her eyes fairly blazed at him.

Brad's mouth snapped shut as if she had doused him with ice water. Jess was right, she might be his pretty cousin, but she was tough and she had proved herself in Alaska and the Amazon. It was at that instant he realized he would not be able to keep Vicky from going along either. These two females were tough, smart, reliable, and stubborn as hell.

When she was certain Brad was not going to try to argue with her, Jessica continued.

"We don't have any idea what the C.I.A. or the State Department is doing about this situation, and we're not going to know until Charlie comes back to the table. So what can we be discussing in the meantime?" She looked around the table.

"We need to figure out routing and transport for the team and gear," Pete said thoughtfully.

"There's no one I can think of at I.C.E. that might know anything of value to us," Vicky said. She pursed her lips and frowned. "I may know somebody in MCISR-E that might know something."

Jessica stared blankly at the redhead. The acronym was something she was totally unfamiliar with. Brad saw her confusion and quickly explained the term.

"MCISR-E stands for Marine Corps Intelligence, Surveillance, and Reconnaissance Enterprise, headquartered at Eighth and I in D.C. They are more strategic planning than operational, though there are personnel there in direct contact with command and ground units. If there is anything to be learned about Murph's situation, it can be learned there."

"If," Vicky said, "and that's a really big if, I can call in a favor or two."

"While we're waiting for Charlie, why don't we watch your recording again, Brad?" Jared reached for the TV remote and switched the DVR on.

"What are we supposed to be looking for?"

"Anything that might give us a clue as to where he is, what faction of DAESH is holding him, what kind of weapons his captor is carrying. Any small detail that could help us plan what to do and how to do it when we get there, Jess," Brad answered.

"There's another thing that's confusing me, Brad. The reporters on television call the jihadists ISIL or ISIS, but you guys all call them DAESH. What's that all about?"

It was Vicky who answered her.

"ISIL and ISIS are acronyms for the Islamic State of Iraq and the Levant and the Islamic State of Iraq and Syria, respectively. DAESH is an acronym for 'al-Dawla al-Islamiya fil Iraq wa al-Sham,' which is Arabic for the Islamic State of Iraq and the Levant.

"It means the same thing, but the word DAESH sounds similar to a derogatory term in the language and the mullahs hate it when it's applied to them, which is the reason why we all use it. By the way, don't use the term when we get there. They don't approve of western women anyway, so it won't take much effort on your part to have some religious fanatic try to cut your tongue out for saying the word."

There was total silence in the room as they watched the digital video recording. When the end of the recording was reached, Jared punched a button on the remote and played it again. The third time through, Jared slowed the speed down to one third normal.

"There!" Jared shouted, leaping to his feet and pointing at the screen.

"What?"

"Watch his eyes! He's blinking!"

Jessica was confused.

"I don't understand. He's blinking. My God, they just hit him in the face with a gun butt."

"It's Morse code," Brad said, his eyes riveted to the screen. "It's a technique taught at SERE (Survival, Evasion, Resistance, and Escape) School. It was used by P.O.W.s in Vietnam to pass information back to the U.S. when they were interviewed by international reporters.

Jared, with his sniper's visual acuity, had spotted Murph's eye movements first, but after he mentioned it, the blinking was plainly visible to them all. He reversed the video and stopped when Murph first appeared. As the man signaled, Jared read off the individual letters.

"Hotel, Alpha, Juliet, Juliet, India, Mike, Oscar, Sierra, Kilo." Murph repeated the message three times, though he was interrupted by a vicious butt stroke in the middle of the third repetition. Jessica felt a rush of admiration for the battered man as she watched him spit out a tooth or two along with a bit of bloody saliva and then continue blinking his message.

"Hajjimosk?" Brad asked. "What the hell does that mean?" No one had a clue.

*   *   *

Murph sat with his back against the rough concrete block wall, facing the door. He winced as his tongue probed the broken stubs of his teeth where the bastards had knocked them out. Despite the pain in his mouth and all over the rest of his body, he was smiling. His captors made a mistake ... actually, they made more than one.

When they led him outside, he counted the steps he had taken once he was outside the building they were holding him in. If they had been competent, they would have put him in a vehicle and ridden him around for a while before they removed the black bag over his head. They had not. They frog marched him almost thirty paces from the building and then they knocked him to the ground. The men had kicked him when he was down and then one of them roughly ripped the bag off his head.

Murph had attended the Corps SERE School at Camp Gonsalves, Okinawa, Japan when he had been sent there to train at the Jungle Warfare Training Center. He learned a lot at the Center, and he volunteered for SERE school afterwards when one of the candidates had been unable to attend. He breezed through the survival portion of the course, but the escape and evasion phase exposed him to situations he had never given much thought to.

During the classroom portion he had been given a lecture, delivered by a former Marine who had been a P.O.W. in Vietnam. The elderly gentleman had still been fit and hard looking even though he was in his 70s, and his lecture had been spellbinding. It had also been enlightening and provided him the technique he had just used against his own captors.

Murph was a proud professional, and his preparation for Operation "We Are Coming, Nineveh" had been exhaustive. There were far too many mosques in the city for him to have been able to recognize them all, but the Mosque of the Prophet Jonah had been one of the most famous. And he had not forgotten the before and after photographs he was shown on the projector screen during one of his briefings.

That particular briefing also included a few interesting facts about the famous mosque, including the fact that, after it was destroyed by

DAESH in 2014, the ruins had been the temporary headquarters of Deputy Leader of Islamic State (IS) Fadhil Ahmad al-Hayali. Hayali, also known as Hajji Mutazz, was killed in an attack on his car in Mosul in 2015. When the hood had been torn from his head, he instantly recognized the famed ruins.

When he saw the reporters arrive in their protected convoy, he remembered the lecture from the elderly gentleman at SERE School. His mind raced as he frantically sought any tidbit of information he could transmit to the cameras by blinking his eyes in Morse code. Very quickly he had come up with a way to give his location in a quick message ... provided someone watching the report was bright enough to figure it out. In the end, he decided to transmit "Hajji" for Hayali, and "Mosk" for mosque. It wasn't much, but it was all he would have time for.

When one of his guards butt stroked him during the interview, he had been afraid that someone had noticed him blinking in Morse code, but apparently it was done strictly for show. Still woozy and bleeding from the blow, Murph spat out the bits of broken teeth and a mouthful of bloody saliva and then continued to blink the code letters. It hadn't been much, but he hoped someone would catch it.

FIVE

Charlie returned to the dining room, and everyone stopped talking and stared at him expectantly. He did not have good news.

"Belus has changed hands again. Jack Rainey sold out to a guy named Stephen Porter. Nobody seems to know a hell of a lot about Porter except that he's a retired Marine Corps light colonel."

There was a groan from Jared, who simply shook his head and shrugged before turning his attention back to Charlie.

"Porter," Charlie continued, "is dragging his feet over the issue of repatriating Murph. As far as Porter is concerned, recovering Murph is a non-issue. Right now he is far more concerned with Belus being under fire from State Department investigators because of allegations of serious misconduct by C.I.A. contract managers. If Murphy has to rely on Belus to pull his ass out of the fire, he is S.O.L." S.O.L. was gruntspeak for shit out of luck.

The stunned silence was broken by another groan from Jared, followed by a bitter remark.

"That low-down quartermaster REMF sonofabitch!" Jared looked sheepish after his outburst, but he sensed it required an explanation.

"I knew Porter back in the day. He was 1st Brigade quartermaster when I was still a buck sergeant. I took a round in the side making a night crossing of the Euphrates in April of '04 when we were ordered to prepare for a massive assault on Fallujah. I unassed all my gear, including my Barrett, to keep from drowning. Somehow I managed to reach the bank and crawled out of the river. My spotter didn't make it, I never saw him again.

"The wound was a through and through, and I was declared fit for limited duty less than two weeks later. They wouldn't let me return to my unit while I remained on a medical profile calling for light duty, so I got stuck at battalion headquarters as a kind of permanent charge of quarters. It didn't take long after that for Porter to come down from Brigade HQ with a Statement of Charges for upwards of six grand in his hands. I asked him why he brought a Statement of Charges instead of a Report of Survey because the equipment had been lost as a result of combat action.

"Porter's nose went straight up in the air and he got rather vocal about it, giving me an ass chewing for my irresponsibility. I was ready to deck him when the brigade sergeant major happened to walk by the orderly room making his daily rounds. The sergeant major listened to Porter browbeating me for nearly three minutes and then walked into the orderly room and snatched Porter's paperwork out of his hands, ripping it to shreds.

"After that he turned the air blue cussing Porter up one side of the room and down the other. When he was done, Porter was shaking ... and to this day I don't honestly know if the shakes were from rage or from fear, but I'd bet my life it was the latter. Hell, the sergeant major even scared me, and he was on my side.

"I didn't see Porter again, though one of the battalion clerks told me later that he had sent down an Article 15 for my commander to sign. The clerk said the sergeant major intercepted the paperwork and put it in the shredder before dropping it in a burn bag. From what I heard, Porter was reassigned rather than relieved. Guess they didn't want to destroy his career."

The anecdote was the longest speech anyone at the table could ever recollect Jared making, and it obviously embarrassed him. As soon as he finished, he buried his face in his second mug of hot chocolate of the evening.

*   *   *

Vicky only half-listened to the conversation as the others discussed Stephen Porter. She was busy searching her memory for any contacts she might have that could shed any light on the situation in Mosul. She had no contacts of any value in I.C.E., and any of the ones she might have had probably would have proved difficult. Her abrupt departure from the agency had disappointed some and irritated the others.

Her best chance of getting any meaningful information was to reach out to a few of her old contacts in the MCISR-E. The people she knew there were strategic assets rather than field intelligence agents, but one or two maintained access to the type of information she needed. There was one contact, Paul Stark, who she felt relatively certain might give her at least some of the information she needed.

There was a problem with contacting Paul, however, a personal issue. Years before, she and Paul had experienced a meaningless fling over a long, dull D.C. weekend. The man was incredibly good looking and came from an old money family. His looks and his Ferrari had been enough to get her to go out with him. Too much alcohol and a long dry spell in her sex life combined to get her to stay with him over the three-day weekend.

He turned out to be an unremarkable lover in bed and an insufferable career bureaucrat out of bed. She had heaved a sigh of relief when he dropped her off at her own apartment on Monday evening. Paul read more into the weekend fling than she had, and things had been a little sticky between them ever since. For that reason she was a bit reluctant to contact him.

Vicky glanced down at her wristwatch and noted the late hour. She would have to wait until the next morning to try to reach one of her contacts.

*   *   *

The atmosphere around the massive table was tense and oppressive. Frustration was evident in every face, but there was little more they could do until they could gain access to more and better information.

Jared was sitting perfectly still, his face a mask of exasperation as he struggled with the letters Murph had signaled on the video. The letters H,A,J,J,I,M,O,S, and K were printed in big block letters on a yellow legal pad on the table in front of him. Under the letters were a series of hard slashes in pencil and then doodled under with a fine-tipped black gel pen. His fingers were gripping the pen tightly enough that the barrel of the instrument was bending in the middle.

Brad was frustrated as hell, but he had learned over the years that patience, much like sleep, was a surprisingly powerful weapon in a warrior's arsenal. At the moment he was well aware that

Vicky had posed a valid point earlier. If he got ahead of himself and tried to force this mission before he had planned and prepared properly, he would screw it all up ... and Brandon Murphy would be the one to pay.

Brad ran his hand through his close-cropped hair and sighed loudly.

"There's not much else we can do tonight, people. Go home. Get some sleep, I think you're going to need it in the days to come. It may be that someone is already hard at work getting Murph out of the hands of those bastards, but my gut tells me it ain't so. In any case, I'd like for us to meet back here at 0700 with fresh minds.

"Do not, I say again, do not do any electronic research or make any phone calls requesting information. I'm ambivalent about N.S.A.'s ability to monitor communications traffic in this country, but I'm unwilling to risk calling attention to ourselves at this time. Does anyone have any questions?"

"Yes," Jessica said. "Are you going to take your own advice, Brad?"

Brad chuckled.

"You always were a precocious brat cousin! Yes, I'm going to get some sleep, but first I'm going to go over a few things that don't require more information. Things like financing this operation..." His voice trailed off. No one believed him, he was sure, but it was late and 0700 would come early.

*   *   *

Brad held a mug of coffee in both hands and stared at the ceiling. He wasn't really drinking it, it was far too late at night to do that if he intended to get any sleep at all. There was a yellow legal pad in front of him, just like the one Jared had been using earlier.

There were numbers on Brad's pad, lots of numbers. His cell phone sat beside the legal pad, the calculator app glowing on the display screen.

Vicky sat across the table from him, minus the shorts she had put on for modesty's sake before their guests had arrived. The single button she had fastened to preserve some semblance of modesty was no longer serving its intended purpose, and if Brad hadn't been so preoccupied he would have been seriously distracted by her display of tanned flesh.

"I have a little money put away for a rainy day, Brad. If you need it you're more than welcome to it." Her voice sounded soft and low, but she'd gotten his attention.

He turned his head to her as if just realizing that she was there.

"I'm sorry, Vicky, I don't mean to ignore you."

"I know," she said with a sultry smile. "You're worried about your friend, but you really should take your own advice and come to bed."

Brad set the mug down and rubbed his eyes.

"Thanks for your offer, Vicky, but no thanks. I really do have a reserve set aside to keep the business afloat in hard times ... or if I suddenly decide to take a long vacation."

"Ving seems to be concerned."

"He is, but then he's never paid much attention to finances. Hell, he couldn't tell you within a hundred dollars what's in his own bank account."

"He seems to be doing okay," Vicky protested. "He has a nice house, a nice new car, Willona drives a nice car, and the whole family dresses well."

Brad laughed aloud.

"Willona handles the finances. She also runs a business on the side buying and selling antiques, a business she truly has an aptitude for. She started doing that while Ving was still on active duty, and she managed to put away a tidy sum.

"She invested a few thousand dollars in a couple of high risk stocks years ago... Microsoft, Oracle, a few others. One or two didn't pay off, but those two made her rich. I have no idea just how rich, but I'm sure she could buy and sell Jessica's dad and he's rich as six feet up a bull's ass."

"Really?"

"Really."

*   *   *

"When are you leaving?" Willona asked.

"Not yet," Ving answered as he opened the refrigerator door and lifted out the platter of bacon and biscuits. He turned and made for the microwave.

"Give me that, Ving!" she demanded, holding her hand out for the platter. She took it and put it in the oven. "The microwave will make the biscuits all soggy, honey, you know that." She shook her head as she turned the oven control knob to the proper temperature for warming. "You shouldn't be eating bacon this late at night, baby, it's bad for you. One of these days all that grease is going to catch up with you."

"I don't know how much sleep I'm going to get, babe. I'm worried about Murph and I'm worried about Brad. We didn't get paid for going after Delroy and I'm pretty sure that cost a bundle. I'm afraid Brad's company is running out of ready cash. He told us tonight that he's digging into his reserve."

"Sit down, Ving. It's time you and I had a talk."

Ving groaned and sat down at the table.

"How much do you think Brad's company is worth, my darling?"

"I really couldn't tell you, Willona. I know he gets paid a lot for the jobs he's been taking."

"I can give you a ballpark figure, Ving, based on my own observations and judgment."

Ving was paying attention now. Willona was not given to talking with him about money. In all the years they had been married he had never worried about money. His check always went into their joint account and she had handled it. He had a check/debit card and a credit card and he bought what he wanted, when he wanted to buy it. She handled all the payments, mortgage, credit cards, and car payments. It never occurred to him to ask her about any of it. He nodded his head, indicating that she should continue.

"As best I can figure, and I assure you I'm pretty close, Brad's 'company' as you call it, would sell on the market these days for approximately three and a half times annual earnings, plus the cost of any property and equipment he uses for the business. His company is a sole proprietorship, not a corporation. I would conservatively set the value of his 'company' at a little over four million dollars."

Ving's eyes widened comically.

"Jesus Christ, Willona!"

"Don't blaspheme, Ving," she admonished. After a moment she spoke again. "Have you ever considered buying a share in Brad's company, honey? Becoming his partner?"

Ving's eyes widened even further.

"Partner? Jesus, Willona, half of his company would be two million bucks... I can't come up with that kind of money!"

Willona smiled, a Mona Lisa type smile, and she ignored the blasphemy this time.

"You don't have to buy half to be his partner, Ving, you could buy a third or a quarter and still be his partner, and he would just be the decision maker."

"That's still an enormous amount of money, baby. We can't handle that kind of purchase... Hell, we'd have to get a second mortgage on the house..."

Willona's hands crossed on the table in front of her, the mysterious smile still on her face.

"What would you say, baby, if I told you we can buy a quarter of Brad's company tonight, in cash, without even making a trip to the bank?"

The timer on the oven went off and Willona rose to get the platter and placed it in front of him. She didn't mention that their ability to buy into Brad's company remained contingent on Brad being willing to sell.

Ving didn't even look down at the platter, he was staring at his wife, confounded, and he listened as Willona explained for the first time their financial situation. How there was no car payment, there was no mortgage on the house, how she paid off the credit cards every month. Then she dropped the bomb on him by telling him that there was a safe in her bedroom closet, and that there was a million dollars in cash inside it.

Ving sat, dumbstruck, throughout Willona's recitation. When she finished, she asked him if he had any questions.

Ving sat for a moment and then tried to speak, but the words wouldn't come and his mouth snapped shut. It was so comical that Willona was hard pressed not to laugh. Finally, he perked up and asked a question.

"Does this mean I can go ahead and buy my bacon refrigerator?" He had joked for years about buying a refrigerator, filling it with bacon, and keeping it in the garage.

Willona lost it … and came around the table to hug the man she loved so very much.

*   *   *

The doorbell rang. Brad, yawning and a little bleary eyed, got up from the table and walked towards the front door. Vicky came out of the bedroom wrapped in a chenille house robe. "Who could be ringing the doorbell at this time of night?" she queried.

"I don't know. I was just about to come to bed." He walked on over to the door, Vicky close behind him. He opened the door and looked surprised to see Willona Ving standing there with a broad smile on her face.

"Willona!" Brad poked his head out the door to look for his closest friend, but Ving was nowhere in sight.

"He's not with me, Brad. I'm here on business. Sorry for the late hour, but I hope this won't take long." She walked inside without waiting to be asked, they had been friends far too long for that. Willona walked over to the dining room table that the team had so lately vacated and set a briefcase on top of it and sat down.

Vicky hugged her and asked if she'd like a cup of tea or coffee, but Willona declined. Brad sat down at the table across from Willona and asked her what sort of business brought her out at this late hour. Thirty minutes later, Willona climbed into her new BMW SUV without her briefcase, and Brad sat staring at a briefcase full of cash.

He held a handwritten document that stated that he now had a partner that owned twenty-five percent of the company that would be formed the next day, Jacobs & Ving Security LLC. Brad and Ving would be the apportioned partners, and Willona Ving was named in the document as secretary treasurer. The document was witnessed by one Victoria Taylor Chance.

SIX

Brad was still a little stunned from Willona's surprise visit when he woke up and not fully convinced that he hadn't dreamed it. He could hear Vicky moving around in the kitchen, and he could smell the aroma of fresh-made coffee. He climbed out of bed and stumbled to the shower to clear his head. The hot, stinging spray from the shower head helped, and then he shocked himself by turning the water to full cold and forcing himself to stand there until he had goose bumps.

When he stepped out of the shower enclosure, Vicky was waiting for him with a heavy mug of aromatic coffee in one hand and a thick cotton towel in the other. He took the towel from her hand and started drying himself. Vicky watched him with an amused half-smile on her face—she was staring at his midsection.

"What are you grinning at?" he asked good-naturedly.

Vicky cocked an eyebrow and set the coffee mug down on the sink.

"Cold water is not your friend," she observed as she caressed him. Then, as quickly as she had grasped him, she let him go.

"Unfortunately, we don't have time to deal with that this morning. I was just about to wake you. Pete will be here any minute now, he sounded very pleased with himself on the phone." She turned and walked out of the bathroom.

"Wait!" he called. "Did I have a weird dream or do I have a briefcase with a million bucks in cash in my safe?"

"I can't tell you what you dreamed, lover, but there is indeed a briefcase full of money in your safe." Her voice took on a pouting, teasing tone. "If you weren't dreaming about me, I may have to step up my game..."

Brad grinned as he stepped into a pair of blue jeans and slipped his feet into a pair of worn, battered, but clean and very comfortable cowboy boots. He threw a black tee shirt over his shoulder and carried his coffee mug out to the kitchen.

Vicky had gone into his office, so Brad rummaged around in the kitchen for something to stave off the hunger until Ving arrived. He knew better than to try to cook before Ving showed up... Ving invariably went to the refrigerator whenever he came over in the early mornings, even if they were just planning on going for a run.

Remembering Ving's passion for bacon, Brad checked the refrigerator for bacon and eggs. There was an open package of bacon and less than a dozen eggs, which meant that someone was going to have to make a run to the grocery store before everyone showed up.

The doorbell rang, and the door opened immediately afterwards. Pete, like the other members of the team, was family. The ringing of the doorbell was just a formality to let Brad know one of them was coming in.

"Coffee's in the kitchen!" Brad called from the dining room table.

"It always is," Pete said. The big man had a wide grin on his face as he stepped into the dining room from the foyer. He tossed a yellow legal pad covered with his backward slanted handwriting to the table in front of Brad as he passed him on his way to the kitchen.

"I had a little trouble getting us a ride at first," Pete called from the kitchen. He came back in and sat down across from Brad, sipping at his coffee.

"Space Available is kind of hard to come by these days." Space Available is a perk of military service, meaning that military personnel and veterans are permitted free rides on military aircraft when there is space available on board.

"So how are we getting to Mosul, Pete?"

"I don't have it nailed down yet because we haven't got a time frame, but the plan is to catch a hop to Fort Bragg on a C-130 milk run out of NAS Fort Worth JRB (Naval Air Station Fort Worth Joint Reserve Base). From Bragg we can hitch a ride on a C-17 into Al Udeid Air Base (located 20 miles southwest of Doha, Qatar). We can catch a hop for Al Udeid to Erbil International."

Erbil, in Iraqi Kurdistan, was a unique facility. The Iraqi Army was forbidden by law from entering Iraqi Kurdistan. There was a curious mix of Peshmerga, International forces and contractors such as Belus at Erbil, and Pete's contact had been confident that he could slip the team into the mix without arousing undue suspicion.

Brad frowned.

"How long is that all going to take us, Pete?"

Pete shrugged.

"No way to get a firm schedule fixed until you give me an okay on a time frame for departure, Brad, you know that."

Brad grinned and took another sip from his mug.

"I'll give you a departure time today for sure, Pete. If we don't have enough information by the end of the day we'll leave anyway and finish our planning en route."

"But it will be sometime today, right?"

Brad grimaced and then came to a decision.

"Improvise, adapt, and overcome, right?" he said with a broad grin. "Set it up for as late today as possible, Pete. If that's not possible try to get us out as early as possible tomorrow morning."

"Is Vicky still on the secure phone?"

The doorbell rang before Brad could answer, and Jessica and Charlie walked in together.

"What's up, Brad?" Jessica asked as she hugged him.

Before he could answer her, the doorbell rang again and Ving appeared, looking hungry as usual.

"I don't smell no bacon fryin'," Ving growled. "What's a man gotta do to get some breakfast around here?"

"The first thing we have to do," Brad observed, "is to get somebody to volunteer to go to the grocery store. I don't have enough in the fridge and the pantry to feed you, much less the rest of the team."

Ving grumbled an unintelligible response. Jessica sighed and picked her purse up off the table where she had just dropped it.

"Charlie and I will go."

"Better take Ving with you," Brad chuckled. "Otherwise he'll be bitching that you didn't get enough bacon." Ving snorted in response.

"You jist git that griddle warmed up, brother. A man can't think straight when he's hongry!" The New Orleans drawl was something Ving had lost years before, but he laid it on thick when he was clowning.

*   *   *

Vicky hung up the secure phone in exasperation. She had managed to reach several of her friends in both the State Department and in Marine Intelligence. But every time she brought up the subject of Brandon Murphy every one of them clammed up, claiming not to know anything about the situation and promising to let her know the moment they learned anything.

The promises rang hollow in her ears, and she had no doubt that as soon as she hung up the contacts would be reaching out to their superiors to report her inquiry. The realization didn't make her angry; she knew if she was in their positions she might have done the same thing. Her mind racing, she pondered her other options. It would have to be done quickly. NSA might be handicapped by relying on their filters to monitor all communications, but shortly they would have several telephone numbers to use in starting a digital forensic trace back to Brad's phone.

Even with the super computers at NSA it would take several hours to get her location. Brad was pretty savvy when it came to setting up secure communications, and he had hired a professional to route the line through a labyrinth of telecommunications hubs, including several satellite feeds.

The only viable option she had left was one she felt reluctant to use.

Paul Stark had left the Corps for more lucrative employment as a civilian contractor for the C.I.A. shortly before they had separated. He made several attempts to renew the relationship over the ensuing years, but she had rebuffed him gently. If she could find him, she thought she might be able to wangle some information regarding Murphy out of him.

Another twenty minutes passed before she located him in Mosul. It took another fifteen minutes to go through the rigamarole of trying to get a satellite phone number for him. The call was brief and very disturbing. Paul had seemed genuinely happy to hear from her, even after she told him she was working with Brad.

He listened to her attentively for a minute or two, but the moment Vicky mentioned Belus, she detected a slight chill in his attitude. She pushed on anyway, but when she mentioned Brandon Murphy, Paul became livid. His tone became so coldly furious that she was taken aback ... until he repeated a code word they had used on their last operation together. The word was so out of context that there was no mistaking its meaning. It meant it was possible that their conversation was not secure on his end.

After the second time he used the word, and he used another code word, the name of an imaginary boyfriend, she realized it meant that she was to contact him by secure means. He then used a code word that meant she needed to get in touch with him in person and then ended the conversation with a qualifier code word that indicated "urgent." Paul had a few personality quirks that Vicky found mildly off-putting, but she trusted his judgment, and he was not prone to exaggeration.

*   *   *

The look on Vicky's face set off alarms in Brad's mind as soon as he saw her come out of his office. He'd been sitting at the table, listening to the banter between Jessica, Charlie and Ving, who had returned from their trip to the grocery store and were cheerfully engaged in preparing breakfast. Ving had located a second electric griddle and had three packages of bacon frying, a spatula in his big fist and a song from his childhood on his lips. Jess and Charlie were singing along with him, and the three of them were swaying in unison... It was hilarious and Brad, Jared and Pete were enjoying the show.

Brad rose from the table, concerned, and approached the woman who had become so important to him. The others, enjoying themselves, didn't appear to notice.

"What's wrong?" he asked quietly. Vicky took his arm and led him out onto the back patio. When they were outside, she turned to him.

"Somebody has clamped down hard on Murphy's situation, Brad."

"State Department or Pentagon?" he queried.

"I don't know. Almost everyone I contacted clammed up the instant I mentioned your friend."

"Almost everyone?"

"There was one guy, a man I … worked with once warned me circumspectly that there was a chance our conversation might be monitored. He used code words from our last op together to let me know that and to let me know I need to get in touch with him in person."

Brad noticed her hesitation when she mentioned that she had worked with the man, but he wasn't about to quiz her over a past relationship. Neither of them had been celibate before they met. If anything, her reticence to be open about it irked him a bit. He was not the jealous type, and he had given her no cause to think he might be.

"What makes you think he's going to talk when you get in touch, Vicky?"

Vicky's face scrunched up as she thought for a moment, considering her answer.

"I slept with him, Brad, a long time ago. Is that going to cause a problem?"

"Not as far as I'm concerned, baby, I just wanted to know how much you trust this guy."

"I trusted him with my life in those days, I've no reason to think I can't now."

Brad saw no reason to respond to her assertion, so he just made a gesture for her to continue and listened attentively.

"Brad, Paul seemed to feel his satellite phone was being monitored. If that's true, then NSA is going to be backtracing my call any minute now. I think we're running out of time... We're going to have to get moving, and soon if we want to reach your friend."

Brad reached out to touch her arm reassuringly.

"That phone line is routed through a dozen or more countries and spoofed by several false phone numbers. The guy who set it up for me is a retired NSA digital security specialist and has a doctorate in digital forensics. It was expensive as hell to get it set up, but he assured me that even the NSA's computers would have a hard time tracking it. We have a couple of hours at the minimum and probably more like a day or two ... and that's provided they are already working on it."

"It still worries me, Brad. I may have compromised this op before we even get started."

Brad smiled at her.

"We have time for breakfast, Vicky. We'll get moving as soon as those clowns do the dishes and clean up the kitchen. In the meantime, let's enjoy a peaceful meal and another cup of coffee." He took her by the arm and gently led her back to the dining table. When they sat down with the others, he leaned over to whisper into Pete's ear.

"It's a go, Pete. We leave as soon as we're done here."

Pete glanced down at his watch.

"I don't know how long it will be before today's milk run takes off, Brad, but I'll get on it right away." He made as if to stand up, but Brad stopped him.

"Time enough for that after breakfast, Pete. We can stage at the warehouse... I still have to get our commo situation resolved. We still don't have a clue as to where Murph actually is. If we don't make today's milk run, we'll catch the one tomorrow."

The warehouse was a small one in an industrial park near the Dallas - Fort Worth Airport that Brad owned in the name of a shell corporation that would be nearly impossible to trace back to him. It was not a large building, only a couple of thousand square feet, but it had room, emergency rations, deployment bags, and a cache of enough weapons and munitions to supply the whole team. The weapons safe in his closet was not large enough to accommodate enough for the whole team. "Nobody goes home after breakfast, Pete, we are Mission Go."

SEVEN

Brad had come away from Captain Dieter's offices equipped with enough BlackBerry DTEK60 cell phones to cover the entire team as well as a handful of spares. The DTEK60 was state-of-the-art in secure cellular communications, and Dieter had simply activated them with the numbers Brad's team was already using.

They had crated up all their gear and Pete had driven it out to Naval Air Station Fort Worth Joint Reserve Base (NAS Fort Worth JRB) roughly six miles from downtown Fort Worth as the crow flies. Pete contacted Hank Guzman, an old military intelligence and logistics buddy that Ving had known for over 20 years. He had worked for the CIA and a couple of other government agencies that he was not allowed to talk about, including Brad's team.

Hank was currently working as a civilian logistics specialist for a contractor for the 319th Special Operations Squadron at Hurlburt Field, Florida. Hank managed to wrangle them a ride on a U-28A making a milk run to Hurlburt Field at eleven hundred hours that he was, conveniently, hitching a ride on. The term "milk run" in military parlance is a routine task, usually round trip, carrying mail, paperwork, passengers or cargo from one installation to another.

Brad and the others watched as the U-28A landed gracefully on the runway. It was a specially modified, single-engine military version of the Pilatus PC-12 aircraft owned and operated by the Air Force Special Operations Command for the purpose of airborne intelligence, surveillance, and reconnaissance.

"Beautiful," Jessica said in a low voice.

"Yes she is," Brad replied, "but she's going to be crowded on this trip. Between the seven of us and the crate, plus Hank, she's going to be close to max takeoff weight."

"Maybe over it considering how much bacon Ving had for breakfast," Jared smirked.

Ving, a half-eaten bacon sandwich still in his hand, punched Jared playfully in the shoulder as the others laughed. Playful or not, the punch moved the rangy Texan six inches from where he'd been standing. Ving kept several more of his sandwiches in a map case he carried around his neck. He knew his favorite food was going to be in short supply in Iraq and he was taking advantage of what he had purchased at the grocery store.

A ground crewman holding wands in his hands guided the aircraft to a parking spot off the tarmac and the engine settled to an idle and then stopped. Only then did the passenger door open downwards, and the familiar face of Hank Guzman appeared in the opened door seconds later. He wore a huge grin on his face as he approached Brad and the team.

Hank was familiar with everyone except Vicky, whose black combat coveralls did little to conceal the lush curves of her slender body. Even dressed for war, with her dark red hair tucked up under a patrol cap and her green eyes hidden by some expensive Ray-Ban aviator's sunglasses she was a striking figure.

"Put your eyes back in your head, Hank," Jessica said, laughing. "This is Vicky Chance, our newest team member, and she's joined at the hip with my dear cousin!"

Brad's cheeks reddened a little at the jibe, but Vicky took it in stride. Vicky wasn't really vain about her appearance, but she knew she was beautiful and she enjoyed the reaction she stirred in men.

Cargo handlers wheeled out the small crate that contained their gear and opened the center door of the plane. Both men grunted with the effort of handling the crate, and it barely fit between the seats.

"Somebody with short legs is gonna have to sit in that middle seat," Jared drawled.

Brad laughed.

"And the old man with the pot belly is going to have to climb over the crate to get to the back!" He was teasing Ving, who had grown a small paunch since he retired from the Corps, though it hadn't slowed the massive man down one iota.

"Man's got to have a little energy laid by for hard times," Ving said, refusing to rise to the bait.

"I think it's cute," Vicky said, patting Ving's belly before sashaying up to the open door and climbing into the aircraft. Hank stared open-mouthed as she walked away. Brad was grinning.

"Don't let the looks fool you, Hank! She's as hard as any leatherneck you ever met."

"You're kidding, right?"

"He ain't kidding, Hank. She took a round in the chest down in Peru, and she walked out of there on her own two feet. Not one word of complaint," Ving said admiringly.

Pete grunted in agreement and followed Vicky onto the aircraft.

*   *   *

"So what are you guys up to?" Hank asked.

"Did you hear what happened to Murph?" Brad asked.

Hank nodded. "Shitty deal... Jesus! You going after him?"

It was Brad's turn to nod. "We're bad short on intel, though; but we had to get out of town pretty quick. Our questions were attracting attention from the wrong people and this op is not sanctioned. There ain't gonna be any support for this one ... unless it's after the fact and we've succeeded."

"Man, it's not like you to go into a mission stone cold," Hank said, shaking his head. "But whatever you're doing, count me in. Murph is a good man, and he's a good friend, and I hate those cruel bastards anyway. Special Ops is giving DAESH a hard time, but their hands are tied by the rules of the game. As I recall, an unsanctioned op doesn't have any rules." Hank smiled grimly. "You have any idea how to go about finding out where they're holding him?"

"We have something to go on, but it's iffy. They put him on display for the media..."

"Yeah, I saw that. Saw them cold cock him with a rifle butt, too, the bastards."

"Yeah, well, Murph outsmarted them. He was blinking in Morse code. Jared spotted it. He spelled out H, A, J, J, I, M, O, S, K before they cut away from him and focused on the leader."

"H, A, J, J, I, M, O, S, K?" Hank parroted. "Any idea what the hell that means?"

"Not a clue, but Vicky knows a guy in Erbil who we think knows more about this than we've been able to learn so far. That's where we're headed."

Hank pursed his lips, deep in thought. "HAJJIMOSK," he muttered. "For some reason, that sticks out in my mind. I know there's a connection there, but I'll be damned if I can make it." He sighed. "Whatever... Brad, I'm in if you have room for a tagalong..."

"You sure, Hank? Won't that get you in trouble with the brass at the 319th?"

"I've got leave time coming, Brad. Besides, Murph is a brother, and Marines don't leave their brothers to the not-so-tender mercies of terrorists."

Vicky, who had been listening silently to the whole exchange, held back a smile. The old saying "once a Marine, always a Marine," was more than just an adage to these men, it was a part of their essence. They could no more leave a friend in the hands of an enemy than they could stop breathing. It just wasn't in their nature. Her attention turned to Brad, who was speaking kindly to the grizzled aviator.

"I think we would be better served if we had you in reserve on this one, Hank." He reached into the small carry-on bag that held his passport and his contractor's paperwork and drew out one of the spare BlackBerry cell phones. "The team numbers are already stored in here. We can use it to contact you if we need some help ... and we need you in the rear where you have access to resources we won't have with us. Trust me, your role in this is more than a shooter."

Hank was visibly disappointed, but he accepted Brad's decision. Then he perked up suddenly.

"Hey Brad, you remember Bob Lingenfelter?"

"Captain Lingenfelter? The Green Beanie we hooked up with in Fallujah?"

"The very same, only it's Colonel Lingenfelter now, a full bird, and I hear he's up for his first star. Anyway, he's the senior adviser to the Peshmerga ... and one branch of that in particular near Mosul that may be of enormous help to you." Peshmerga translates literally as "facing death". They are military forces of the portion of Iraq known as Iraqi Kurdistan. Technically, the head of the Peshmerga is the President of Iraqi Kurdistan.

The force itself is loosely knit, split up and regulated by the Democratic Party of Kurdistan and the Patriotic Union of Kurdistan, both of which are pledged to the government of Iraqi Kurdistan. The splintered groups of Peshmerga forces are in charge of protecting the land, people, and traditions of Iraqi Kurdistan because by law the Iraqi Army is forbidden entry into the region.

Brad leaned back against his seat, sifting through his memory for facts about Peshmerga. He spoke Arabic fluently, as did Ving, Jared, and Charlie, all of whom had attended the Defense Language Institute Foreign Language Center at the Presidio of Monterey Army Garrison, host installation for the school.

None of them that he knew of were fluent in Kurmanji, Sorani or Palewani (the three principal Kurdish languages), though they were all familiar with a smattering of words and phrases from having occasionally worked with the Peshmerga during their tours in Iraq.

"Shit!" He looked around. "Does anybody speak Kurmanji, Sorani or Palewani?"

"I speak Kurmanji," Vicky said quietly, "and a few words of the other two … enough to get by."

Brad was about to ask her a few questions regarding the Kurds in general when Jessica shocked him by speaking up.

"I speak enough of all three to get by, but I'm not fluent." When she saw Brad's astonishment, she offered an explanation. "I spent six long months in Kirkuk, trying to locate an ancient Assyrian treasure that was supposed to be hidden beneath the ruins of the Kirkuk Citadel."

She went on to explain that Kirkuk was built on the site of the ancient Assyrian city of Arrapha, and the citadel itself was located in the center of the oldest part of the city. The citadel was built on a man-made mound nearly 130 feet tall on a plateau across the Khasa River.

Brad sat in his seat, speechless. He had completely forgotten Jessica's expedition to Kirkuk. He was livid when she told him, after the fact, that she had been gallivanting around on a treasure hunt in a war-torn country, but since she returned without incident, he had promptly dismissed it from his mind. Jessica was nothing if not headstrong, and nothing he could have said would have persuaded her to stop her pursuit of legendary treasure once she researched it and decided she had discovered something no one else had.

Her fearlessness, however, had not turned out to be of the reckless kind. She had proven in Africa, Alaska, and Peru that she was reliable and effective under fire, and the other members of the team fully accepted her as one of their own. She was turning into a far more valuable asset than he could ever have imagined.

* * *

The slender U-28A landed at Pope Field in the early afternoon, its slender fuselage dwarfed by the C-130s and C-17s in the pattern and on the ground at one of the busiest military airports in the world. Pope Field had transitioned from the U.S. Air Force and been incorporated into Fort Bragg early in 2011. The aircraft did not proceed directly to the refueling point; rather it stopped temporarily on a concrete apron off the end of the runway.

Anyone observing would have seen seven people come out the passenger door, two of whom, a massive, bald black male and a heavily muscled white male, proceeded to the center door on the fuselage and removed a rather heavy narrow wooden crate. The whole group then walked a short distance before stepping onto the cargo ramp of an idling C-17, disappearing inside. The ramp rose, and the giant aircraft immediately moved onto the ready line.

Minutes later, the huge C-17 lifted off the runway and began its steep ascent into the bright blue sky. Its final destination was Erbil, Iraq, but on the way it would land and refuel at Morón Air Base in Andalusia, Spain.

EIGHT

Despite their extensive travels in Iraq and Afghanistan, none of them except Hank and Vicky had ever been to Erbil. Every one of them was astonished at the modern city revealed in the windows as the giant C-17 transport landed. Erbil sits on an arid plain, and the only real difference they could tell from the air between Dallas and Erbil was that all the roofs looked flat, even the residential ones.

"Jeez," Jared observed. "If I didn't know better I could swear I was looking at the outskirts of Dallas or Phoenix."

"It gets a lot colder here than it does in Dallas," Vicky said, laughing, "but it doesn't rain much. The wind blows so hard and so much in winter that there's little snow accumulation to worry about, it's constant here."

Instead of remaining on the tarmac to unload, the massive transport was waved into a huge hangar and the crew chief made them stay in their canvas webbing seats until the engines were shut down and the hangar doors were closed. Then the tailgate lowered and he allowed them to debark. A ridiculously neat man wearing a freshly pressed khaki suit and dark sunglasses appeared waiting for them on the smooth concrete floor. A cord ran from inside his suit jacket up his neck to an earbud.

*   *   *

Warner F. Jenkins III had majored in political science at George Washington University in pursuit of his dream of a career as a diplomat. An incident occurred in his junior year involving an excess of alcohol and a letch for a freshman girl who turned out to be the daughter of the civil service examiner who was responsible for vetting his application after he graduated. As a consequence, his career hopes had been blasted to smithereens.

He had been more fortunate when his application to the C.I.A. had been vetted, and he had been hired as an entry level targeting officer. Directorate of Operations (DO) targeting officers plan and implement foreign intelligence collection, counterintelligence, and Covert Action operations. Entry level TOs have to learn and gain experience in operational tradecraft to identify and develop new opportunities for operational activity and to improve and support current and future operations. Jenkins had been in the Middle East for nine years.

He had been more than a little irate when his supervisor, Duncan Willingham, handed him this "babysitting" assignment. Willingham, an Ivy Leaguer with a smarmy Boston accent and an insufferable superiority complex, had bluntly told him that the civilians he was to babysit were busybodies involved in something way over their heads. He found the assignment demeaning to say the least, but he wasn't paid to like his job, just to do it.

The first member of the group to exit the tailgate of the C-17 caused him to have the pleasant thought that this assignment might not be as dreary as he had anticipated. A slender redhead with a dynamite body and a walk that would make a dead man sit up and take notice headed straight towards him, and he felt his mouth go dry. She was followed by a slightly taller blonde who was pretty damned good looking, too, and his hope rose.

The next three members of the group set off alarm bells in his head, big time. Brad Jacobs, Mason Ving, and Pete Sabrowski were heavy hitters in an industry known for its highly skilled professionals. Their reputation for effectiveness and their success rate were legendary at C.I.A., and their faces were well known to him. He had never met any of them, but he had read their dossiers. For the first time in his career, he was impressed.

"Vicky Chance," the stunning redhead said as she extended her hand to shake his. Her grip felt surprisingly strong and firm. His heart was pounding as he looked into her incredible green eyes. He became so overwhelmed that he almost didn't notice the tall, lanky cowboy who stepped out of the aircraft next.

Another heavy hitter, a sniper with a storied and colorful career in the Marine Corps, Jared Smoot. Jenkins smelled a rat. This group was not comprised of "busybodies." Whatever they were here for was serious business, and he should have been warned. The only thing that seemed to contradict his considered opinion was the presence of the two attractive females.

Brad, Ving, and Pete had closed with the trio and Brad was first to offer his hand.

"Hi, I'm Brad Jacobs, what do you have for us?"

"Huh? I know who you are, I just... Huh?"

"You look like a Company man to me... I figured somebody at N.S.A. had figured out what we're up to and alerted C.I.A. I assumed you were here to share what information you have concerning the whereabouts of Brandon Murphy."

"Oh Jesus!" Jenkins was shocked to his core. "This is not good..."

"What's the matter?" Vicky asked.

Jenkins glanced around the hangar and then beckoned Brad and the others to follow him. He led them to a glassed-in room at the far end of the hangar that had the words "Break Room" carved into a wooden board hanging from the steel entry door. He waved them nervously into the metal folding chairs around the Formica topped lunchroom tables and then began to pace back and forth, running his hand through his close-cropped, sandy-blond hair.

"I'm not believing this!" Jenkins cried.

It was Ving who broke the confused silence.

"Would somebody please tell me what the hell is going on here?" he boomed. His eyes were going flat, and he was building up a fine head of steam.

"Spill it, buddy. Ving is getting pissed, and, trust me, the one thing you do not want to do right now is piss off my large friend." Brad's eyes were steely as he stared at the sweating C.I.A. operative.

"Listen," Jenkins said, "I know you guys, most of you, by your reputations. I just can't believe they would do this to you ... to me..."

"What the devil are you talking about?" Vicky snarled, sensing trouble. The transformation in her pretty features was fearsome.

Jenkins sank down into a folding chair next to Brad and clasped his hands in front of him.

"I'm not sure what's going on," he murmured. He turned to Brad. "Until you mentioned Murphy, I had no idea what you and your team were doing here. I was told to bring you into this break room and stall you as long as I could... I wasn't told anything about your group being involved with Murphy. Jesus, why would they keep that from me? Why would they want me to sequester you in this damned hangar?" He rested his head in his hands.

Brad leaned back in the chair, his brows furrowed in thought.

"So what are you supposed to eventually do with us? You had to know we weren't going to stay here, no matter what they told you..."

Jenkins sat up straight and put his hands on the table.

"I'm supposed to take you to a PAK unit almost thirty klicks east of Mosul some time near midnight."

"What the hell is a 'PAK' unit?" Brad asked.

"It's part of the Peshmerga," Vicky remarked. "They have nearly six hundred or so fighters loyal to the Kurdistan Freedom Party, known by its Kurdish acronym, PAK."

"I'm not sure I understand," Brad said quietly. "Why would they want us with Peshmerga and why east of Mosul?"

"The boss doesn't have much respect for this particular unit," Jenkins said. "He thinks they're ineffective despite the reports we're getting of their successes in the field."

"Sounds like he wants us to get bogged down with some real losers," Ving observed.

Jenkins' shoulders slumped as the implications of his assignment hit him full force. His job was to sandbag a group of highly respected civilian contractors and keep them from doing what they came to do, rescue Brandon Murphy. But the big question remained—why?

Vicky remained sitting up straight, her back rigid, her fists clenched on the table. She turned to stare at Hank.

"Are you thinking what I'm thinking?"

"The women?" Hank asked.

Vicky nodded and turned back to Jenkins.

"Is that it? Are we being sent to the women's unit?"

Jenkins nodded.

The smile that slowly spread across Vicky's face appeared cruel and hard.

"We caught a break, Brad. His jerk of a boss is a chauvinist idiot."

Brad's brows rose in question.

"DAESH is scared shitless of those women," Hank interjected. "I hear those women sing into loudspeakers before they make an assault. The jihadists believe they will be denied Paradise if a woman kills them … and, trust me, these women kill, and they like it." The comment was the last one Hank contributed before Jenkins reluctantly ordered the security team to let him leave the hangar to report in to his supervisor.

"Most of them have lost a family member to DAESH, a husband, a child, a parent. Their strength is in their hate." She looked at Jenkins. "What kind of idiot has the C.I.A. put in charge here?"

Jenkins shrugged miserably.

*   *   *

Just after ten, local time, the lights inside and outside the hangar were extinguished and the big sliding doors of the hangar opened. A large, flat, black carryall entered the building and the doors quickly slid shut behind it before the lights were turned back on.

The team remained sitting in the bay with their backs to the wall, field stripping and cleaning their weapons, loading magazines or sharpening knives. None of them were wearing utilities or camouflage; they were dressed for combat in an urban area, jeans with cargo pockets and dark woolen hunting shirts. The civilian clothes were Brad's idea.

Fatigues, utilities, and camouflage were the order of the day in Mosul, on all sides of the crazy conflict. There were so many players... Americans, British, Aussies, the Iraqi Special Forces, Germans, Canadians, Peshmerga. Then there were the DAESH jihadists from Iraq, Afghanistan, Syria, and

Iran. There were so many players it would take a scorecard to keep up with them.

A plan was forming in Brad's head, one he had been constructing with advice from the members of the team. Each had unique abilities and skills, and each had something to contribute. Jared, reassembling the CMMG M4 with its eighteen-inch stainless bull barrel that he preferred for in-city sniping, was the one who had baldly stated the obvious.

The only way they could beat the odds stacked so badly against them was to treat the mission as a standard P.O.W. snatch—a diversion and a fast, hard surgical strike. No one mentioned the problem that was bothering them most of all; they still didn't have a clue as to where Murph was.

Brad and Vicky had grilled Jenkins thoroughly, and the C.I.A. target officer had repeatedly denied any knowledge about the Murphy "issue" as he referred to it, though he had been noticeably troubled by the questions. He was openly relieved when they stopped questioning him.

"He's holding back," Brad murmured to Vicky as they watched Jenkins suck down a bottle of water and then mop his face with a large, white bandana.

"Yeah, he knows something, Brad, I just can't figure out why he won't tell us. You could see how uncomfortable he looked when he realized who you were. He's holding back all right, but he doesn't like it."

Brad scratched his head. "No doubt about it." He stared at the ceiling for a moment. "What possible reason could the Agency have for sandbagging us, Vicky?"

It was a long time before she responded.

"I don't know, baby, but I'd bet money that Paul Stark knows about it. That would explain why he refused to talk about it and insisted on me meeting him in person."

"I know we have to do it, but I still haven't figured out how you're going to manage that, Vicky."

It was a moment before she answered him.

"I'm going to call him and tell him to meet us as soon as we arrive at the PAK site east of Mosul."

"You realize that by now they are monitoring his calls. If you use the new secure BlackBerry, they may not be able to decrypt it, but they're going to be able to get a fix on your location."

She nodded. Then she smiled.

"Yes, probably, but they already know we are here, don't they?"

Brad tried to counter her logic.

"Vicky, we don't have a firm location on the PAK site yet."

Her smile became sly.

"We don't, but he does!" She pointed at Jenkins. Then she unfastened two buttons on her shirt, reached up to let her hair fall and primped it, and then stood up and walked over to the hapless Jenkins.

Brad grinned. The poor sap had no idea what was about to happen to him. Vicky could be very persuasive.

NINE

The ride in the carryall was not very comfortable, crowded as it was with the team and their gear. The carryall's body appeared rough, bearing the dents and dings of years of abuse. But underneath its disreputable looking steel skin existed a thoroughly modern chassis and enough armor plate to protect the passengers from any but the most powerful of small arms fire. Ving and Pete were the most uncomfortable because of their size and the interminable time it took for the trip over the horribly inadequate roads.

In daylight, under normal circumstances, the trip would only have taken an hour and a half. Jenkins experienced a conscience attack and had finally given them a map instead of driving them as he'd been ordered to do. Brad suspected that the TO was going to lie to his superiors, telling them he had been forced to remain behind. But he didn't care as long as Jenkins waited long enough for them to get out of Erbil first. Ving had "persuaded" Jenkins to cooperate with Brad's wishes. The man had been positively terrified.

There were roadblocks and checkpoints marked in pen on the map, necessitating the negotiation of goat trails and, on one occasion, the fording of a fairly deep stream. By the time they reached the PAK camp, the first rays of the sun began peeking over the horizon.

The encampment was a surprise, a small, neat tent city in the hill country nearly 30 klicks (kilometers) east of Mosul. The city was surrounded by dug in, revetted positions and all the tents were sandbagged. The perimeter sentries looked alert and aggressive at a time when most humans were at a low point in their circadian rhythm. Their alertness was a testament to their discipline and their leadership.

The team was stopped and searched by a gaggle of wary sentries at the entrance to the camp until the commandant, a surprisingly svelte lieutenant colonel in tailored fatigues, was brought to meet them. She was accompanied by a petite captain who looked as if she should have still been in high school. Neither woman was veiled, a fact that surprised everyone but Vicky.

She had seen these women, or others like them, the last time she'd been in Erbil, and she knew that many of them had gone to the extreme to throw off the yoke of their ISIS oppressors. Discarding the veils was a sign of open defiance. Still, many others wore the veil in deference to their own personal religious beliefs, but all wore the sand-colored camouflage uniforms of the Kurdistan Freedom Party.

The colonel had a distinct, no-nonsense military bearing, and she looked the team over as if they were recruits before she spoke. When she did speak, she spoke in English with a startling and pronounced British accent.

"I am Lieutenant Colonel Ester Goran, and this is my adjutant, Captain Besna Pashew." She did not offer to shake hands.

"Who is the leader of this ... group?" she asked. It seemed clear from her tone she was not impressed by what she saw. The tiny captain appeared to be fascinated with Jared. Ving's nostrils flared and his eyes narrowed as he studied the woman, but the other team members inclined their heads toward Brad.

"I'm in charge," he answered calmly.

"I was opposed to your C.I.A. sending armed strangers into my camp, but the PAK commander has ordered it. My adjutant or another officer will remain with you at all times during your hopefully brief stay with us. You will be treated civilly, but you must understand that we are in a very precarious situation here and cannot afford to trust anyone. Any of your people who are found wandering around the tent city unaccompanied will be taken into custody by any means necessary. Have I made myself clear?"

Her little speech sounded clearly rehearsed and her vocabulary was that of a highly intelligent person who had formally studied the English language.

"Understood." Brad hesitated a moment. "We may need to bring in one more person..."

The colonel's eyes flashed as she struggled visibly with her temper.

"I was not informed of this!" she said through gritted teeth. She looked as if she was going to break into a real leatherneck style ass-chewing, but the morning stillness was broken by the unmistakable sound of an incoming mortar round.

"Incoming!" Ving roared, diving for cover even as he spoke. Even as the others hit the dirt the concussion and the blast from the mortar round washed over them. Brad and Vicky were low-crawling towards a sandbagged position around a crew-served machine gun when Brad felt a small hand tugging on the leg of his faded denim jeans.

He turned his head to see Captain Pashew shaking her head "no" and stared at her in confusion. Three more incoming rounds impacted in or near the position, and then Brad understood. He screamed at Vicky and got her turned around and moving away from the machine gun emplacement and towards a revetted sentry post twenty feet in the other direction. There were scattered hits all around the tent city by then, and then total silence.

"Oh shit!" Jared's voice rang out. Even Jessica knew what was coming next, though she had never experienced it. The attackers had a spotter nearby, and they had obviously gotten the range. Sure enough, after the brief lapse, the number of incoming rounds dramatically increased as the mortar crews began to "fire for effect".

Following Pashew, Brad crawled into the revetment, dragging a reluctant Vicky behind him. His lungs were burning from unconsciously holding his breath, and he had a foul taste in his mouth. The acrid odor of HE (the high explosive used in the mortar rounds) wafted over the compound as the hellish nightmare continued. Vicky knelt close by him in the revetment as Brad did a quick visual survey from the relative safety of his position.

The bombardment had taken a terrible toll on the women of the PAK unit before they managed to get to cover. The uniformed bodies of the female warriors lay scattered around the area, some still and silent, some bleeding and moaning. One woman was sitting up holding the stump of her arm, trying frantically to stem the flow of arterial blood.

Before he could stop her, Vicky was out and running towards the soldier. Brad wanted desperately to go with her, but he forced himself to stay and finish his visual check on the other team members.

Jessica and Charlie had reached cover, and they were working furiously to aid several of the wounded PAK women in their shelter. Ving was with Colonel Goran in the guard post bunker at the tent city entrance. The colonel was shouting orders into an old EE-8 field telephone. Jared was low-crawling along a ditch leading to the fence, for what purpose Brad could only guess. Pete was absolutely nowhere in sight.

The whole survey had taken only seconds. Satisfied that he had done all he could, Brad crawled out after Vicky, and together they dragged wounded woman back into their revetment. Brad glanced down at the woman's bloody breast pocket to see if it bore a name tag, but there was none. Vicky started whispering reassuringly to her, but Brad couldn't hear a word she was saying.

As suddenly as the bombardment started, it stopped. There was no sound but the cries of the wounded and the bawled orders of the non-coms. The loud report of a rifle shot and a shout penetrated the deafening silence rudely, and Brad's eyes were drawn to Jared, who had taken up a prone firing position beside a spot of low elevation in the security fence.

He leaped to his feet.

"Dallas! Go!" he shouted, unslinging his CAR-4 from his shoulder and racing over to support Jared. He used the word "Dallas" because he knew that his team members would recognize the word and respond. His own words were ringing in his ears, and he couldn't be sure that the others would recognize his voice. It wouldn't occur to him until much later that he had finally given his team a name, but from that moment on the PAK women referred to the team as "Dallas."

Brad dove to the ground about five meters to Jared's left and got into a prone firing position. Roughly a hundred meters in front of the fence he could see two hundred or more hostiles making their way towards the encampment, armed to the teeth.

The team joined him on line, spread out in prone positions to either side of Brad and Jared, their weapons barking. No one was trying to be a hero. Their shots were aimed, squeezed off one at a time; a disciplined, precise, and effective tactic that slowed the advance of the hostiles. Wild-ass full auto fire looks good in the movies, but the truth is aimed fire is far more frightening—and deadly— to a foe. Anyone who has ever fired a shotgun shell into a flock of birds can testify to it.

*   *   *

Jessica stumbled and fell to the ground a few feet from Jared, and out of the corner of her eye she saw Charlie hit the ground hard. He was already firing while she kept trying to sight in on her first target. She had gotten two shots off when one of the shells coming out of the ejection port on Jared's rifle struck the back of her neck and slipped down inside her shirt.

The damned thing felt hot, and it burned her skin, but she didn't jump up, she merely whimpered and slid to her right. Bullets from the hostiles were already whickering and buzzing like angry hornets over her head. It would have taken more than a startling burn to make her raise her head so much as an inch.

*   *   *

Pete had been last to reach the team. He had come from behind a sandbagged tent, holding a handkerchief over his ear. One of the mortar rounds in the initial bombardment had struck right next to him and the concussion had been strong enough to knock him off his feet. Miraculously, none of the shrapnel from the blast hit him, but the concussion put enough pressure on his left ear to cause it to bleed.

He had lain, stunned, on the ground for just a moment before two small PAK women dragged him behind the sandbag wall of their tent. It had been one of their medics who had given him the white handkerchief. As soon as he'd been able, he had gotten to his feet, unslung his rifle, and rushed to the aid of Brad and the others. He couldn't hear his own rifle firing.

*   *   *

Despite bringing steady and accurate fire to bear on the advancing DAESH troops, it looked obvious to Ving that the team was never going to stop so many of them. He was pleased to see many of the Peshmerga women firing alongside of them, and they were shooting like professionals instead of amateurs.

Nevertheless, far too many of them had been wounded or killed in the intense mortar attack, and the hostiles were still coming. Raising his head, he looked left and then right. Around twenty feet from where he lay, there was a sandbagged position for a crew-served weapon. The uniformed bodies of three Peshmerga soldiers were draped lifelessly over the sandbags.

Low crawling had never been his forte, so he scurried in a bear crawl to the emplacement. To his surprise, the weapon itself did not seem to be damaged. Even more surprising was that it was an old surplus M-60 machine gun mounted on a tripod. The M-60 was an old friend, as familiar to Ving as his own hand.

With a hasty mental apology, he shoved the three bodies off the sandbags and knelt down behind the weapon. He lifted the cover assembly, twisted the ammunition belt and tossed it aside. Then he slid the bolt back with the cocking handle, inserted a fresh belt, slammed the cover down, and slid the cocking handle forward.

When he sighted in on the advancing hostiles and pulled the trigger, the bolt slid forward and he heard one of the most beautiful sounds any grunt could ever hear—a sweet three-round burst making the distinctive sound of the M-60. Satisfied that the weapon was fully functional, Ving fired a longer burst, watching the projectiles kick up dirt and stone as he walked the rounds into the front ranks of the hostiles. When the first batch began to fall, he switched back to six-to-nine-round bursts and proceeded to rain down hell on their comrades. His fire was devastating.

The bolt locked to the rear after he expended the first two-thousand-round belt, and he quickly lifted the cover. Before he could reach for another box, a small, brown hand slipped a cloth bandoleer over the cartridge feed tray assembly and laid the first round neatly onto the feed tray. Swiftly Ving slammed the tray cover down and began to fire. The little Peshmerga trooper had a tight grim smile on her lips as Ving began to fire again. Ving was a regular artist with an M-60.

*   *   *

When the shooting was over and the hostiles had finally retreated, Jared got to his knees and began to collect the empty thirty-round magazines beside him. He put them in the cloth claymore bag he carried the loaded magazines in, and then picked up the camel-colored Stetson hat that he wore everywhere except to bed and placed it squarely on his head.

He heard a giggle behind him and turned to see three of the PAK troops behind him. None of the three were wearing veils, and one of them looked remarkably pretty. In his cowboy boots, faded jeans, western shirt, and Stetson, the rangy Texan was a rare and forbidden temptation for the dedicated freedom fighters.

They had been raised in a society that could punish a woman for simply being alone in a room with a male who was not their husband. The recently liberated among them found Jared with his friendly, easy-going manner and ready smile much to their liking.

He grinned at them and began to walk towards where Brad and the others had begun gathering around Ving, who seemed to have found an M-60 to adopt.

*　　　*　　　*

"Everybody all right?" Brad asked. He reached out to tap the handkerchief at Pete's ear, but the man pulled away.

"I'm okay," he said thickly, "just can't hear very well right now."

Looking into Pete's eyes, Brad spoke slowly and clearly.

"Do you need to see a doc?"

Pete started to shake his head and then thought better of it as a dull pain throbbed in his head.

"Nah. One of the PAK medics looked at it. I'll be all right soon as my head quits ringin'." His eyes rolled up, and he said almost prayerfully, "Jeez I wish I had a cold beer right now." All the others laughed quietly, but he didn't hear them. Alcohol was prohibited in Iraq, at least the kind you could drink.

*   *   *

Colonel Goran, with Captain Pashew once again dogging her footsteps, came over to where the team was gathered. She spoke to Jared first.

"I'm curious, cowboy. What made you go to that particular spot on our perimeter? And why did you go when the mortar assault was over?"

Jared's Texas drawl grew thicker when any woman seemed to be paying particular attention to it, and the colonel was a fine looking woman, even if she was an officer. He took his forefinger and tipped his Stetson back on his head as he cradled his specially modified CAR-4 in his free arm.

"It's been my experience, ma'am, that a mortar attack is usually a diversion created to soften you up before an all-out assault. As far as why I picked that particular spot, it's the lowest point in your perimeter with a downhill approach that offers concealment." Jared pulled a toothpick from the hatband of his Stetson and slipped it between his lips. "If I was you I'd have a few of these ladies clear up some of that brush after the bad guys collect their dead."

Colonel Goran pointed at what looked like a company of soldiers forming up just inside the gate. A trailer that looked suspiciously like a water buffalo marked with the Arabic script for "gasoline" appeared hooked up to an old three-quarter-ton Dodge pickup truck painted in a sand camouflage pattern parked behind the formation.

"They will not come back for their dead or wounded. DAESH believes that if a man is killed in battle by a woman, he is disgraced and he cannot enter into Paradise."

"So they're going to collect wounded prisoners and bury the dead?" Brad queried.

"There will be no prisoners," Captain Pashew said flatly.

"But … the wounded…" Jessica spluttered.

"There … will … be … no … prisoners," Pashew repeated in the same flat tone. Then she turned and walked away.

Jessica stared after the diminutive captain half in anger and half in dismay.

"I can't believe—"

"What?" Goran asked. "That she could be so callous?" Jessica nodded. "Do not judge her too harshly. DAESH beheaded her husband … after they stoned her daughter to death in front of him. She was very devout before that happened." She turned to watch the grim-faced soldiers as they marched out the gate towards the downed hostiles.

As soon as the company cleared the gate another company formed up and followed them. After approximately thirty meters, both companies spread out on line, weapons at the ready.

*   *   *

Brad watched, his arm around Vicky's shoulder, as the soldiers closed with the fallen hostiles, individual shots began to ring out and Vicky turned her head towards the colonel.

"She went with them, didn't she?" Jessica was asking about Pashew, but she didn't direct the question at anyone in particular.

"If you are asking about Besna," Colonel Goran said softly, "she is not one of the shooters."

In response to Vicky's raised eyebrow, Goran said something that turned even Brad's stomach.

"It is written in The Quran: *'And We ordained for them therein a life for a life, an eye for an eye, a nose for a nose, an ear for an ear, a tooth for a tooth, and for wounds is legal retribution.'*" Goran locked eyes with Vicky. "Besna carries with her in a canvas pouch a heavy stone, three times the size of her fist. It is one of the stones that was used to kill her daughter. She will not use her rifle to dispatch the wounded soldiers of DAESH."

"Jesus…" Brad muttered under his breath.

Vicky remained watching Goran very closely.

"Captain Pashew is your adjutant, but you seem to know an awful lot about her personal life," Vicky remarked.

The colonel remained silent for a moment, as if she was deciding whether to respond or not.

"Captain Pashew is not merely my adjutant," she responded finally. "She is my daughter. The child DAESH stoned to death was my granddaughter."

TEN

As he had been taught to do, Murph started each day in captivity with a self-assessment. When he finished, he croaked his evaluation to the shadows in the empty cell.

"Gunnery Sergeant Murphy, sir! Present for duty, but pretty fucked up." Then he chuckled at his own humor. He would not have remained a gunny in the Corps for very long if he'd ever reported to an officer that way. Even so, he had spoken the truth.

They made their first mistakes the day after they captured him. Taking him outside and removing his blindfold without disorienting him first had been inexcusably stupid. Afterwards, the two men who brought him back to his cell had been so busy amusing themselves by beating and kicking him that they had not bothered to search him. His face had been more recognizable before that, probably so that he would be more presentable for the television camera crew.

When they'd made him grovel in the dirt, his bound hands had closed on a roughly made, bent and rusted nail, which he managed to conceal by dropping it down inside the waistband of his jockey shorts. He used the nail to scratch small lines on the wall behind where he normally rested his back to keep track of days. It was harder to keep track of time locked in a windowless cell.

His face was battered and bruised, and both eyes were swollen, though the right one would still open enough for him to see. His parched tongue constantly probed the broken teeth in his mouth.

That brought to mind another problem. His captors gave him just enough water to keep him alive but nowhere even close to enough to slake the thirst that threatened to drive him mad. He had been extremely careful to remain hydrated since he'd been in-country, but he'd had only a swallow or so each day since he'd awakened in captivity.

The only thing they'd given him to eat was a couple of pieces of the thin, flat bread known as *khubz or khobuz.* It was tough and chewy, and it was used by locals in place of utensils to eat their meals. Very little fat was used in baking the bread, which was basically pita bread, and it was tasteless.

Murph wasn't worried about food, he knew he could last a long time without food. It was the scarcity of water that was going to kill him … if his captors didn't beat him to death first. Apparently, their expressed desire to exchange him for ransom was a joke to them.

That thought brought a crooked grin to Murph's lips. Thus far he had been able to fool them into believing he did not understand them when they spoke. They were wrong. The beatings had actually helped with that. It remained easy to keep from showing emotions or any kind of reaction to their speech when his face and lips appeared puffed-up and bruised.

Although their religious quotes and slogans were in Arabic, they spoke to each other most often in Farsi, both of which Murph had learned at the language school in Monterey. He was fluent enough in Farsi to pinpoint the leader's home town of Tabriz, which told him the jihadists were from Iran. The conversations Murph overheard had already given him tons of intelligence that would be extremely valuable if ... no, when ... he managed to escape from this hellhole.

He groaned softly and leaned back against the rough concrete blocks of the wall. Had anyone caught his Morse code message? Was there anyone watching who would be able to understand the significance of hajjimosk? He knew there were analysts in the intelligence community that would have caught the code. But was there anyone out there who would grasp the meaning of the initials that had been the only message he'd had enough time to blink out quickly? Shit! What if the camera hadn't caught it?

The notion that his message might not have made it onto the film felt terrifying. If it hadn't, the only option he possessed to escape these crazy, vicious bastards was to fight his way out with a rusty, old, poorly made nail that looked bent almost double ... and that would mean he was as crazy as they were.

*   *   *

The chief crazy bastard, Hamid Kavoosi, lay resting on a hard pallet of thin cotton in a room strikingly similar to the one Murphy was imprisoned in. Hamid's room, in contrast to Murph's cell, contained a small portable Sterno stove and a Styrofoam cooler filled with bottled water. The water had been stolen from the relief supplies the American Red Cross had distributed in the part of the city the Islamic State failed to retain. The shame of their failure to hold the outskirts of Mosul burned inside Hamid's body like the sun.

Hamid Kavoosi's father had been a mullah in their neighborhood, a very strict, hard line mullah who had been a rabid supporter of Ayatollah Khomeini. The elder Kavoosi had been martyred in the second battle for Fallujah, dying with the name of Allah on his lips in a rusty, old Peugeot packed with C-4 stolen from the lazy Americans.

The only people easier to steal from than the Americans were the French ... though one didn't have to steal much from the French. The French were more than willing to sell anything the leaders of ISIL wanted since money seemed the one thing ISIS was not short of.

Between the support of elements of the Saudis and the support of the United Nations' aid programs, ISIS had money practically falling out of their robes. More than one of the leaders of the jihad had disappeared into the woodwork with vast sums of money, never to be heard from again. The remaining leaders simply issued a qaḷā, a legal ruling made by a judge (qāḍī) that condemned the offender to death. In any nation where Islamic law is observed, the order is binding. After that, the offender appeared forgotten until some zealot carried out the sentence ... or not.

There sounded a knock on Hamid's door, and he arose from his pallet to greet his visitor. In this case, his visitor was simply another Sunni extremist member of the group bearing his morning meal. Hamid stood, rinsed his hands with water from the plastic bottle, then wiped his face, leaving his hands wet.

Still standing, he accepted the proffered wooden platter, on which rested a Mosul staple, pache. Pache, lamb (and lamb parts, including hooves, brains, stomach, and intestines) boiled in a fatty broth seasoned with lemons and onions and served over a round of *khubz*, is an acquired taste. But it is cheap and easily obtained locally.

He ate the simple meal carefully, tearing the bread and using it to wipe up the pache. He was paying close attention as he did not wish to fail to be in the proper state of mind for *Salat al-Fajr*, the first prayer of the day between dawn and sunrise.

Later, after saying his prayer and performing a few routine administrative tasks, he dutifully checked his rifle, an M-16 he had personally taken from the body of an infidel *Yazidi* in Sinjar, a small town on the border between Syria and Iraq. He allowed himself a thin smile of pleasure. Those crazy Americans! They kept arming the faithful in the Middle East and they had no idea. It was no wonder their interference was doomed to failure.

He strolled out into the dim corridor to check on the infidel before checking on his men. Thinking of the prisoner brought another smile to his lips, a much wider one. The smile, however, did not extend to his eyes. His eyes reflected the same blazing fanaticism they always did. The smile receded into a smirk as he neared the door of Murphy's cell.

He had taken the prisoner as a lark, intending to provide a little sport for his men, who had experienced some unsettling setbacks of late and sorely needed a little entertainment. The orders from higher up had come as a disappointment to him, but Allah had commanded him to be obedient. So he had taken the American before the reporters with their television cameras and demanded a ransom so outrageous that Hamid knew his government would never agree to pay.

Even if the impossible happened and the Americans handed over the ransom, it would not be necessary to keep his side of the bargain. Nowhere in the Holy Quran did it say he could not deceive infidels. He could hand over the man's body just as easily as he could give him back alive;

alive or dead was not specified in the wording of his ransom demand. Then his men would not only have the money, they would have the pleasure of removing another unbeliever as well.

Hamid arrived at the door to the infidel's cell and greeted the guard he'd posted by the door.

"Salâmun 'alaykum!" he said, using the proper declension of the phrase to include all the members of their group, even though they were not physically present in the hallway.

"Salâmun 'alaykum!" came the correct response. Their sect rigidly obeyed the laws of Allah, peace be upon him, and the proper greeting and response were specified in the Quran. It remained the considered opinion of Hamid and the hierarchy of the sect that modern Islam had been corrupted and that it was their obligation to see that all Muslims obeyed the laws.

Hamid reached up and slid back the shutter that covered the observation window to the cell, gazing at the infidel.

"Has the infidel been fed as I instructed?" he asked without looking at the guard.

"All has been done as you instructed, agha," the guard replied. Hamid's instructions had been precise and detailed. The prisoner's water bottle was to contain only enough water to moisten his mouth, and the server was to hand it to him with his left hand only.

A mortal insult to any Muslim for the left hand is the one favored by *Shaitan*. When the prisoner had swallowed the water, a small piece of *khubz* was to be torn from one of the flat, round loaves, again using the left hand, and the bread was to be tossed on the concrete floor of the cell.

Murphy was leaning against the far wall of the cell, his battered and swollen face a grotesque mask of pain and misery. Even from across the room it appeared clear that his bruised lips were dry and chapped, but it was also clear he seemed in no danger of imminent death … just yet.

Very pleased, Hamid thoughtfully reconsidered his order for the infidel to be guarded around the clock. The walls were of rough concrete block. The only exit was the thick steel door, which remained locked from the outside with a massive high security padlock to which there existed only two keys, one of which remained on Hamid's person at all times. The other key was passed from guard to guard as they changed shifts.

The past weeks had been grueling and morale had been slipping. The fighters needed to regain their strength and bolster their spirits. The guard duty was merely a custom, and Hamid decided on the spot that it had become unnecessary. The infidel was weak, and there was nothing in the cell that could be used as a weapon.

He held out his hand to the guard.

"Go, agha. Give me your key and go. See to the needs of your body and see to your prayers. The infidel is going nowhere."

The guard gratefully acknowledged Hamid's reprieve from the onerous duty of guarding the prisoner. He handed the key over with an obsequious half-bow and hurried away to join the other jihadists.

Hamid pocketed the key and promptly turned to gaze through the thin slit of the observation room once more. The prisoner had not, to his knowledge, made any effort to pray to his heathen god, nor had he insisted on being permitted to cleanse himself. He deserved to be treated like a dog. Sliding the cover back over the slit, Hamid turned and strode away, secure in the knowledge that the infidel was thoroughly intimidated.

His disdain for Murph was an extension of his contempt for all who resisted the goals of the Caliphate ... for all infidels. His dedication and his attitude set a fine example for his men, and it generated the same contempt in his troops.

His treatment of the prisoner also salved the pain of their initial losses to the infidels in the invasion of Mosul, and it bolstered the morale of his troops. If the prisoner got dinged up a little in the process, it was no skin off his nose. As far as he was concerned, his superiors would find no fault in him if the prisoner didn't survive his confinement long enough to gain the ransom money. The money was tainted anyway, and he was doing Allah's will. How could they fault him?

The prisoner was not a threat, he could not escape. There was no need to leave a guard on the secure cell, it would be sufficient to have someone check in on him every few hours. Besides, no one, not even Hamid's own superiors, knew precisely where he was being held. Everything was going as planned.

ELEVEN

Besna Pashew's countenance was impassive when she passed back through the entrance to the tent city. Her eyes were stony, and she seemed eerily zombie-like. The other women were all still outside the perimeter fence, stacking the bodies of the dead into piles preparatory to burning.

Her hands held a blood-spattered stone, and her camouflage uniform was covered with drying blood. No one spoke to her or paid any attention to what she was doing, as if her behavior was normal. Unlike the other women, her M-16 had never left her shoulders as the wounded were dispatched. Vicky noted that Colonel Goran watched Pashew cross the compound through lidded eyes before turning her attention back to Brad and the others.

Ester Goran seemed an impressive figure of an officer, but there was something behind her eyes that told Vicky she was holding something back ...

something important. Even as the colonel was praising what she was now calling "Team Dallas," there remained a reserve in her manner that struck Vicky almost forcefully. Brad was dutifully paying attention to her, but Vicky took the opportunity to look around at the PAK soldiers.

Female though they were, the soldiers went about their duties in the same manner as their male counterparts. They were clearly a disciplined and highly efficient organization. Medics appeared busy caring for the wounded, and line troops were bearing stretchers over to a triage tent.

Other soldiers were hastily replacing sandbags damaged in the attack, while still others scrutinized the perimeter fence for damage. The whole scene was an impressive display of discipline and efficiency, something Vicky had rarely observed in any of the Middle Eastern organizations she had worked with or around. It was almost ... unsettling.

"There is something more going on here than meets the eye," she muttered under her breath.

"What?" Jessica asked quietly. The two of them were standing a couple of paces behind the rest of the team, paying little attention to the little show being played out in front of them.

"Nothing," Vicky said softly. "Just talking to myself."

Her attention was drawn back to the colonel by the arrival of a sloe-eyed beauty of a sergeant who wore no veil and was dressed in an uncharacteristically form-fitting camouflage uniform. Her fatigues were tailored, even better than the colonel's, and she was blatantly flirting with the men of the team, who were not at all immune to the woman's charms.

There was a shout from outside the perimeter, and all heads turned as flames spouted up from the piles of bodies, followed by a pall of black smoke.

Colonel Goran called for an orderly and then ushered the team back towards the TOC (Tactical Operations Center), which was her field headquarters. Her stated purpose was to offer refreshments to the team as the cleanup continued, but it seemed clear to Vicky that the real purpose was to distract them. She touched Jessica's hand lightly and motioned for her to hang back a step or two as the group moved toward the TOC.

"I'm going to visit the latrine in a few minutes. I need you to come with me to distract our escort. I have to make a phone call and I don't want these people to know about it," she whispered. Jessica bobbed her head in understanding.

*   *   *

"Why are you whispering, Vicky, and where the hell are you? I've been going crazy wondering where you were!"

"I'm whispering because I'm in a PAK latrine and I have a keeper outside who is supposed to be watching my every move! Now shut up and listen to me because I haven't much time." She recited the grid coordinates she had taken from the display on the DTEK60. The fact that Goran had not ordered them searched and the cell phone confiscated was a surprise to her, considering the professionalism displayed by Goran and her troops thus far.

"Read it back to me, Paul," she ordered. When he was finished, she spoke into the cell phone once more. "That's almost a half hour outside Mosul. Can you get here?"

"You're with that all female PAK unit?"

"Yes Paul, now answer the damned question! I told you, I don't have much time."

"Jesus Christ!" Paul said in exasperation. "Listen carefully to me, Vicky. Somebody way above my pay grade is doing everything they can to sandbag your op. You and your friends are in deep shit! Stay right where you are, and do *not tell anybody* you have spoken to me today. Got it?"

"Yes," Vicky answered, shaken.

"Good. I'll be there within the next couple of hours." The cell phone went dead in her hands. Stunned, but grimly determined not to keep Brad in the dark about contacting Stark, she carefully washed her hands with the water bottle and left the latrine.

Jessica was standing exactly where she had been when Vicky entered the canvas walled latrine, loudly chattering away at their escort, speaking in Kurmanji. The escort had been pleasantly surprised to find the pretty blonde American spoke her language, after a fashion, and she had been easy to distract.

Jessica kept up the chatter as they strolled back to the TOC. The conversation was sprinkled with laughter whenever Jess butchered a word or phrase in Kurmanji, which was often. Vicky walked behind them, silent, her mind racing.

Paul Stark might have been lousy in bed, but he had been an exceptional intelligence officer. He had an uncanny knack for getting information he was not cleared for, and he had a near eidetic memory. And he clearly had information regarding Brandon Murphy that was not common knowledge.

He also appeared to have detailed knowledge concerning an effort to keep Brad and his team out of the picture. That was a major problem and Brad needed to know about it. The challenge Vicky faced was getting him far away from Colonel Goran and that sultry sergeant long enough to tell him the news.

Vicky wasn't insecure enough to feel jealousy over Brad's distraction. The woman was certainly exotic and earthy, and she definitely exuded a blatant air of sexuality, a distinct oddity amongst Middle Eastern women. She was, however, absolutely irritated with Brad for being so susceptible to the sergeant's charms. She expected more of him.

*   *   *

The sergeant, whose name was Azade, still had the men of the team in the palm of her hand. Her hip was cocked to one side and she had thrust her full, firm breasts out invitingly as her hands traced arabesques in the air. A good storyteller always makes use of their hands to give emphasis to their stories, and Azade was an excellent storyteller.

Jessica was more the jealous type than Vicky, and she wasted no time in taking up her place beside Charlie when they reached the TOC. Her smile of greeting to her lover looked more a grimace than anything else, though she made no effort to take his hand. To have done so before the PAK women would have been a disastrous cultural gaffe, and Jessica was fully aware of that. She did manage to grind her heel down on his toes surreptitiously, which brought a genuine smile to her lips and a slight smirk to Vicky's.

Colonel Goran missed the little display, but Brad did not. He glanced first at Jessica, and then at Vicky. With a barely perceptible inclination of her head, Vicky signaled for Brad to move closer to her.

Before he could move, Colonel Goran spoke up, interrupting Azade's little show.

"I'm sorry to interrupt this little conversation," she said apologetically, "but I have to see to my personnel. Azade will see to it that you are fed and made comfortable, and we shall meet later to discuss your purpose for this visit." Her smile rang false as she thanked them again for their performance in the defense of her compound, and then the group watched as she strode off in the direction Captain Pashew had taken.

Moving subtly, Brad maneuvered around to the back of the group where Vicky stood with her arms folded across her chest and then took a knee. He took several of his empty magazines out of the claymore bag hanging from his shoulder and laid them out on the ground. Then he began to noisily reload the magazines one round at a time. A brief look of annoyance crossed Azade's face, but it didn't interrupt her little show.

"Contacted Stark," Vicky muttered out of the corner of her mouth.

"And?" Brad continued reloading.

"And somebody high up the food chain is trying to keep you away from the Murphy situation."

"Shit! Any idea who?"

"No. I gave him our coordinates, he said it might take him a couple of hours to get here."

Brad raised his head and looked up at Vicky, noticing the set of her jaw.

"Are you pissed at me?" he whispered. She neither returned his gaze nor answered. At that moment Azade asked them all to follow her to a tent that had been hastily set up to accommodate them.

The tent was a surplus U.S. Army issue GP Medium with the "U.S." stencil painted over it. Inside, the dirt floor had been covered with thick carpets, which Jessica seemed fascinated with. In the center of the carpet rested a small charcoal brazier holding a dallah, a traditional Arabic coffee pot used for centuries to brew and serve Qahwa, a type of spiced Arabic coffee. Beside the brazier sat an oblong platter holding several flat round loaves of *khubz*, a bowl of some unrecognizable paste, and a small mound of dates.

A veiled PAK trooper knelt and poured the coffee into tiny cups before presenting them to the team. When she was done, she made a graceful motion with her right hand indicating that they should eat, and then she went outside the tent to kneel beside Azade at the open doorway. She did not take her eyes off them for an instant.

"Eat," Brad commanded brusquely, "and don't do it with your left hand." The advice about the left hand was unnecessary because they had all been in the Middle East at one time or another and were familiar with the custom and the reasons behind it. It did, however, serve as an indicator of Brad's mood.

They were all still in a somber mood from the ruthless dispatching of the assault troops despite Azade's efforts to lighten the mood and distract them. Ving, who knew Brad better than any of them, intuited what his partner wanted.

He patted his claymore bag, now filled with empty magazines instead of the bacon sandwiches he had stored inside at the beginning of the trip.

"Dadgum," he said ruefully. "I knew I shoulda saved back some of my sammiches." He bent forward and tore off a chunk of *khubz* then dipped it into the bowl of meat paste before lifting it to his mouth and smacking his lips. The others followed suit, talking and eating. The conversation was innocuous, but it gave Brad the cover he needed to talk with Vicky.

"What's up with Stark?" he whispered. She answered in a whisper, telling him everything Paul had said to her except that he had told her not to tell Brad.

Brad sat back on his heels, trying to imagine a possible reason for the C.I.A. to freeze him out of his attempt to rescue Murph. There was no way the Company or the State Department was going to accede to the ransom demands, that much was official U.S. policy. That left the possibility that a rescue operation might already be in progress, in which case Brad needed to butt out before he got somebody killed.

There were other possibilities, but he couldn't think of any. He cursed in frustration then calmed himself. He needed a clear head to make good decisions. Closing his eyes, he began a set of deep breathing exercises, and by the time he had finished, a clear, logical plan had formed in his mind.

"We can't make any plans until Stark tells us what's going on, so we need to do what we have the resources to do until he gets here. I don't think you can get Goran to talk, but Pashew has a weakness we can exploit."

Vicky arched an eyebrow, asking a silent question.

"She's running on hate, Vicky. She wants to hurt DAESH any way she can. It's personal for her, and

I think we can use that to get her to tell us what Goran is keeping from us."

"And how are you going to do that, Brad?"

Brad's smile was tight lipped.

"I don't think she'll talk to a man ... but I think she'll talk to you and Jess."

*   *   *

They found Besna Pashew squatting alone by a crew-served weapon emplacement that had taken a direct hit. She was staring at the twisted remains of an M-60 and the torn and blood-spattered sandbags that surrounded the position, her eyes blank and vacant. Vicky and Jessica squatted beside her, but neither of them knew how to begin the conversation so they remained immobile and silent, staring at the ruined position with her.

Vicky realized with a start that there was something curious about the mortar attack. The initial impacts had been remarkably accurate, striking the sandbagged emplacements with a precision unusual in mortar fire.

She reviewed the beginning of the attack in her mind, reliving the terrifying moment of that first explosion and the almost instant "fire for effect" after the initial rounds impacted and detonated. In that instant she gasped as she reached an incontrovertible conclusion. DAESH had known the precise location of every crew-served weapon emplacement, down to the inch. Not only had they been able to strike with pinpoint accuracy, someone had been within eyesight of the camp to confirm the placement and order the mortars to "fire for effect".

Pashew heard her gasp and knew that Vicky finally comprehended what she had known from the first.

"Yes," she said dully, "we have a traitor in the camp."

Jessica inhaled sharply.

"You knew?" Vicky asked, though she already knew the answer.

"So many lives taken from us," Pashew said softly, ignoring the question. "So wrong. Are we not all followers of the Prophet? In my heart I know this is not what Allah intended ... and I believe he weeps for what is done every day in his name."

The captain turned her head to one side and said bitterly, "I can no longer weep, my tears have been exhausted. First my daughter, then my husband. Every day since has been filled with the blood of friends, relatives, innocents ... and every day since my heart has been filled with hate."

She stopped and slowly turned her head to face Vicky. "With all your power and all your wealth, you Americans cannot stop what is to come. Islam will prevail in the end. The only question is which version will still exist when it happens, the true faith or the perverted form practiced by DAESH." She spat the word DAESH out like an expletive.

Vicky chose her next words carefully.

"You know we are not representatives of our government."

"Your government is involved in this matter whether you represent them or not," Pashew said sullenly. "We would all be far better off if it were not for the interference of outsiders who have no understanding of our ways and of our faith. Be warned, you have no friends here." She closed her mouth as if she realized she had said too much. She said nothing more.

*   *   *

Paul Stark did not arrive at the tent city within two hours. The late afternoon sun was setting when his nondescript black van arrived at the entrance, and he was quickly dragged out of the front seat and forced to lie face down in the dirt. The sentries, augmented by several soldiers from nearby gun emplacements where they were rebuilding, started shouting and aiming their weapons at him. One of the PAK soldiers climbed inside the van and began to search it.

Another PAK soldier began to pat him down, and seconds later there was excited shouting from the group surrounding him. A handgun of some type was tossed out of the ring of women surrounding Stark and at nearly the same time a shout came from inside the van.

"Shit!" Brad exclaimed. He recognized the Kurmanji word for "spy". He left the tent in a headlong rush, followed by the rest of the team. By the time he managed to get moving, the hapless Stark was being mauled by his captors.

"Stop!" Brad roared in Kurmanji. He waded right into the midst of the furious women with Ving and Pete close behind him. By the time Vicky and the others reached the melee a few seconds later, the women were pointing their weapons at the three men as well as their new captive. They were mad as hell, and their suspicion was plain on their faces ... at least the unveiled ones.

Several of the troops turned and faced the rest of the team, weapons at the ready should they try to free the four men in the center of the ring. The situation was about to degenerate into all-out war when a shouted command from Colonel Goran froze everyone in their tracks. All eyes turned to the slender woman who stood with her clenched fists on her hips, glaring at them with all the dignity and majesty of an Old Testament avenging angel.

TWELVE

The tent they had been taken into as guests had turned into a makeshift prison. Stark's van had been driven inside the compound and parked outside the tent, its keys safely in the pocket of Colonel Goran.

Stark, battered and bruised by the sentries, sat between Vicky and Jared on the thick carpet, eying the brazier and the empty platter wistfully.

"I never got a chance to eat today, and I'm starved."

"We'll take care of your stomach later," Brad growled. "Now tell me where those assholes are holding Murph."

"I don't know," Stark said simply. "And what you need to understand is that it doesn't matter anyway."

"What the hell do you mean 'it doesn't matter'?" Ving asked, his face a mask of fury.

Stark shook his head sadly and answered him slowly and succinctly, as if he were speaking to a simple child.

"Because you're never going to get within a mile of the guy. The word is out, orders from on high. Jacobs and his pals are not to be permitted to interfere with this operation. Period. End of story."

"Operation?" Pete asked in confusion.

"Murph was allowed to be captured as part of a C.I.A. op?" Brad was pissed, and it was obvious.

"No," Stark responded, "he's just part of the cost of doing business as far as the Company is concerned." He shook his head. "You people have no idea what you've gotten yourselves into."

Ving looked ready to strangle the C.I.A. man. "Enlighten us," he demanded.

Stark thought for a moment before deciding to answer.

"The asshole running the little band of freaks who captured your pal Murphy is Hamid Kavoosi, a real nutcase. He and his men take special assignments from the higher-ups in DAESH, troubleshooting jobs."

"So what do they want with Murph? Why is he so special to them?"

Stark chuckled.

"That's the hell of it. Murphy was an accident. DAESH has no interest in him at all; even the ransom demand is a joke. They don't need money, they have cash practically falling out of their asses. Between the Saudis, the U.N., and our flippin' commander-in-chief, those guys are rolling in dough." He shook his head sadly. "Face it, Jacobs, your pal is as good as dead."

"So why does the C.I.A. want to keep me from snatching him away from Kavoosi?" Brad demanded.

"You still don't get it, do you?" Stark's tone was mocking. "Kavoosi and his mopes are all Iranian, and their first loyalty is to the Ayatollah, not DAESH."

"Damn it!" Jessica cried. "The carpet! The freakin' carpet!"

"What the hell?" Jared asked, staring at the slender blonde in bewilderment.

"Something about this carpet has been nagging at me ever since we came into this tent. Now I know what bothers me."

They all waited in silence for her to continue.

"I recognized it," she explained. "This is an Isfahan carpet! You can tell by the designs and the pastel colors, very unique." Isfahan, Iran, is famous for the high quality of their rugs, which are fantastically expensive, even in the Middle East. For a Peshmerga lieutenant colonel to have access to one in a temporary camp was totally absurd. It was an indication that she was either a person of considerable wealth, which was unlikely, or that she had friends in high places who were.

"Colonel Goran in league with the Iranians?" Vicky asked. It was a rhetorical question. It made sense, it would explain how DAESH knew the precise locations of the weapons emplacements ... and why they did not bother to target the TOC.

*   *   *

Brad sent Vicky, Jessica, and Stark to sit in front of the entrance to the tent to provide a distraction for the guards, who had definitely lost their admiration for "Team Dallas".

Brad, Ving, Pete, and Jared sat in a loose circle, hoping to come up with a tactical plan to get them out of the tent city and into Mosul. They still had no idea what they were going to do once they reached Mosul. None of them had a clue yet as to what Murph had meant when he blinked his "hajjimosk" message, but it really wouldn't make any difference if they couldn't get out of the PAK compound.

The PAK women had searched them and taken their weapons, but they were evidently not as familiar with western weaponry as they should have been. Brad's belt buckle was in actuality a small, razor sharp push knife. Jared always carried a thin spring steel blade sewn into the side welt of each of his beat-up cowboy boots. Ving and Pete were so massive that neither of them bothered to carry anything concealed, their ham-sized fists had always served them well. The discussion was kept at a low volume as they carefully assessed their situation.

*   *   *

In front of the entrance to the tent, Jessica had fallen asleep and lay on her side, her face resting on her hands. Vicky and Stark were talking in English instead of the Arabic the group had been conversing in throughout the day. They couldn't be certain, but it was unlikely that all of their captors spoke English.

"You know, don't you, that you can kiss your career with the C.I.A. goodbye after coming out here to help us..." Vicky was saying.

"You left me no choice, Vicky. Hell, you know I still have feelings for you..."

She shook her head sadly.

"I'm off the market, Paul." She inclined her head back toward Brad. "He's the *one.* I was really attracted to him from the beginning, but I didn't really realize how much I loved him until I went back to D.C. after the Amazon mission."

Stark sighed heavily.

"I would have come anyway," he said. "I've been party to an awful lot of dirty tricks the Company loves to play, but this was the straw that broke the camel's back. Honest to God, I can't tell what side I'm even on any more. There is something definitely wrong with this scenario, I smell a rat."

"Unless they figure out a way out of here, none of it matters, Paul."

"There aren't *that* many guards on this tent, Vicky. We could take them in a rush later when they start to get tired and less vigilant."

"No doubt Brad and the others have considered that, but it would still leave us with no way out of the camp. They would mow us down before we could reach one of their vehicles, and they took the keys to your van, I saw Goran put them in her pocket."

A slow smile spread across Stark's face.

"You've underestimated me again, Vicky." He dipped his head toward the left side of the tent. "That shabby old van out there may look like it's on its last legs, but underneath that ramshackle exterior lies a gen-you-wine spookmobile."

Vicky's green eyes widened in surprise.

Stark reached into his trousers pocket and took out a green dyed rabbit's foot on a short chain. With his thumb, he flicked the top to one side, revealing a small, red button and a small, white button sitting side by side, before flicking it back shut just as quickly.

"The white button is a remote starter. One push on that button will light up a state-of-the-art, fuel injected, high-performance V-8 engine from up to a hundred feet away."

"What's does the other one do?"

Stark put the rabbit's foot back in his pocket.

"Boom!" he said, straight-faced. "Underneath the gas tank, surrounded by armor plate that will become shrapnel when the time comes, is thirty pounds of C-4."

"Jesus Paul! Brad needs to know that!"

"So tell him."

"Wake up Sleeping Beauty there, Paul, and get her talking. I'll go back and tell Brad. This might be the one element he needs to put together an escape plan."

Vicky waited until Jessica was up and engaged in an animated discussion with Stark before she stood up and walked back to Brad and the others.

Brad scooted over to make room for her to sit beside him, and she sat down cross-legged between him and Ving.

"How's it coming?" she asked conversationally, keeping an eye on the guards, who were watching Stark and Jessica suspiciously.

"We've figured out a way to overcome the guards, but everything we can come up with to get out of the camp is downright suicidal. We're going to have to make a break for it, Vicky, but I'm not sure any of us is going to make it." He raised his hands helplessly.

"Stark is a bringer of gifts," she whispered. She quickly told them what Stark had said about the van.

"No shit?" Jared asked excitedly.

"No shit," she replied. "Now calm down before the guards get leery." She turned her head back to Brad. "Now tell me the plan."

*   *   *

Brad called out for Stark and Jessica to come back to the center of the tent. They did so slowly as the guards watched nervously from outside. He waited for them to sit down before he spoke.

Softly, he restated the information about the van for Jessica's benefit. Then he outlined the escape plan.

"I really don't want to kill any of them," he cautioned after he had explained what they were going to do, "but we do what we have to. This isn't going to work until the wee hours, so what I want you to do now is stretch out and try to catch a couple of winks. I'll wake you up at the right time. Remember that sleep is a weapon."

"But you'll have to stay up, you won't get any rest," Vicky protested.

Brad grinned and tapped the chronograph on his wrist.

"I have an alarm, Vicky, and, besides, if we're all racked out the guards are going to get lazy. When it's time to go, those women are going to get the shock of their lives."

Pete made a grumbling noise deep in his enormous chest.

"Yeah, probably gonna shock 'em wide awake so they can slaughter us all."

Ving burst into laughter, startling the guards, before clapping Pete on the back.

"Come on, Marine, you wanna live forever?" He was quoting Sergeant Major Daniel Joseph Daly, an Irish American United States Marine who had yelled, "Come on, you sons of bitches, do you want to live forever?" to the men of his company before leading them in a charge against the German lines during the Battle of Belleau Wood in World War I. Daly had received the Congressional Medal of Honor for his actions that day.

It was warped humor, but the team found the quip hilarious. As the apprehensive guards watched, they stretched out on the thick Iranian carpet and tried to sleep. Brad sat up a bit longer, setting the alarm on his chronometer. Then he laid back, placing his hands behind his head, and fell asleep.

*   *   *

The chronometer's alarm woke him at zero two thirty hours, and Brad instantly opened his eyes and gazed out at the guards. One of them was actually sitting cross-legged on the ground, drowsing. The other was still on her feet, but she was swaying slightly as she stared sleepily out into the darkness.

Brad rolled over and patted Vicky awake, holding his finger in front of his lips to keep her from talking. Beside him on his other side, Ving sat up and lightly tapped Jared on the shoulder. He had dozed, but very lightly. Charlie was a little harder to wake up, but not much. Neither Pete nor Jessica had slept much, and they were both clear headed as Brad and Jared bared their blades and concealed them behind their backs. Stark hadn't slept a wink.

"Ready?" Brad whispered.

As one, they gave him the thumbs up signal and crept quietly toward the front of the tent.

"Go!" Brad whispered hoarsely before he leaped through the broad entrance of the GP Medium tent. He clapped one hand over the mouth of the standing guard and pulled her to the ground as Ving did the same to the one dozing. Stark, rabbit's foot in hand, raced around the tent toward the black van. As soon as he rounded the corner he encountered another sentry and he swung wildly at her with his free hand, knocking her senseless to the ground. Vicky, right behind him, leaped onto the sentry's partner, who had raised her weapon and was about to scream a warning.

Vicky had no choice, placing both hands around the sentry's head, she gave a sharp twist. The sound of the sentry's neck snapping was audible in the semi-darkness of the tent city, and Vicky felt a sickening sensation in the pit of her stomach.

Stark opened the front door as quietly as he could manage, and climbed into the front seat. Vicky tried the latch to the cargo door, and, finding it unlocked, slid it back for the others to enter before climbing in. They were all inside before a shout came from a spot near the gate. Stark thumbed the white button and the powerful engine roared to life.

A PAK major, Goran's executive officer, clambered out of the bunker by the main entrance at the same time that Colonel Goran and Captain Pashew exited a GP Small tent, apparently Goran's quarters, rubbing their eyes.

They were taking sporadic fire, the rounds striking the van with awful thuds, when Brad pointed towards Goran and Pashew and shouted for Stark to stop the van beside them. Stark thought Brad was insane, but he obeyed the incredible command without thinking about it, slamming on the brakes and locking the tires so that the van slewed and skidded to a stop.

Ving, instinctively discerning Brad's intentions, jumped out of the van while it was still shuddering to a stop and grabbed the two women in his massive arms. He tossed them through the open cargo door and dove in on top of them, screaming for Stark to get moving. The gunfire increased dramatically as Stark raced toward the gate, even as the major shrieked an order to cease fire to avoid hitting the colonel. She had watched in horror as the huge black man had seized her and thrown her into the van as if she was a rag doll.

The sentries blocking the reinforced wire gate either didn't hear the cease fire order or refused to obey it, stood their ground and fired directly into the front of the oncoming vehicle. Stark didn't swerve or slow down, he struck the sentries hard, sending their smashed and broken bodies flying before slamming into the gate and then through it.

Jessica, still holding tightly to one of Jared's thin blades, barely heard the bullets peppering the back door of the van. She was scared to death, but she was alert. As the van hurtled down the dark dirt road, she felt a heavy weight crash into her legs. She looked down in the dim light of the interior to see Pete slumped against her, his broad face twisted in pain.

THIRTEEN

Brad had felt a bullet tug at his plaid shirt just before the van had rolled over the body of one of the dead gate sentries. He had ducked instinctively just in time to see a hole appear as if by magic in the crown of Jared's Stetson. The wide-brimmed hat fell to the bare steel floor of the van, but Jared didn't appear to be hit.

Stark didn't fare nearly as well. Once they were through the gate, he slumped forward over the wheel, groaning loudly in pain. Brad snatched him from the driver's seat, pushing the wounded man into Vicky's lap, as Jared hopped into the seat and then stabbed the gas pedal with his right foot. The van rumbled off into the darkness.

Brad stared anxiously out the broken back window of the van, but there was no sign of pursuit yet. He turned back toward the front of the van.

"Status check!" he barked.

"I'm good," Jessica yelled. "Pete's hit!"

"I'm okay," Ving said, "but the colonel is in a bad way." He continued trying to stanch the flow of blood from several holes in Goran's chest, but he already knew she was a dead woman, even if her body didn't know it yet.

"I think I need to change my drawers," Jared yelled, "but I ain't hit."

Brad took a quick look at Pashew, who was trembling and staring at her dying mother but appeared otherwise unhurt. Then he turned to Pete to see if there was anything he could do to help. Jessica was pressing a blue patterned bandana against his thigh, just below the spot where he'd been hit on the Amazon mission.

"It's a through and through Brad," Pete said through clenched teeth. "Didn't hit the bone, but it hurts like a bitch!"

"Help me get Paul to the floor," Vicky called out.

Brad crept forward, swaying with the motion of the heavy van, until he reached the right front seat. His eyes met Vicky's and she shook her head. Stark was in a bad way, but she wasn't going to be the one to confirm it for him. Together, they dragged him past the now dead Goran and the cowering Pashew to an open spot on the floor. The ride was bumpy as hell, but they made him as comfortable as they could.

It was Charlie who knelt down beside Stark and leaned close to him as Brad and Vicky worked frantically to stop the bleeding from his chest. Stark's breaths were coming in gasps, and an ugly sucking sound was coming from him. Vicky jumped up and opened the top of the van's center console, looking for something suitable to seal a sucking chest wound.

She returned with a soft plastic sandwich bag that still contained the crumbs from some snack that had long ago been eaten. She turned the bag upside down and shook the crumbs out onto the van's bare steel floor. Then she turned the bag inside out and wiped it on the leg of her safari pants before slapping it down over the nasty hole in Stark's chest. The gruesome sucking noise stopped immediately, but his breathing was still labored.

"We need to know where they're holding Murphy," Charlie was saying. "All we have to go on is something he signaled to us on the news camera, he sent 'hajjimosk' in Morse code."

Stark tried to laugh, but he choked and an ugly bubbling sound rattled in his chest. "Hajjimosk?" he asked, before trying to laugh again. Slowly and painfully, between labored gasps, he explained the significance of the word, of how Hajji Mutazz had been beheaded in front of the Mosque of the Prophet Jonah. "That's got to be it! That's where the crazy ... bastard is holding him ... can't believe

... didn't recognize ... the ruins." He kept wheezing badly. "Nineveh," he gasped. Then he passed out.

Brad frowned. "Is he gone?"

"No, but Goran is," Vicky said, her first and second fingers stretched across Stark's jugular vein, feeling the faint pulse. "But it won't be much longer."

"Nineveh," Charlie muttered.

"Nineveh, the mound-ruins of Kouyunjik and Nabī Yūnus." Jessica said. "It's located on the plain near where the Tigris and the Khosr Rivers meet." She shook her head. "I can't believe I didn't get it. I thought the ruins looked familiar, but I couldn't place them. Maybe if the camera angle had been wider..."

*   *   *

Brad dragged Goran's body to the rear of the van and began the grim process of searching her pockets for anything of intelligence value. Besna Pashew, still shaking, watched him with wide, scared eyes as he performed his grisly task on her mother's body. Before he touched any of her pockets, Brad removed her web belt, which bore a Czech CZ 75 9mm pistol in a holster as well as two ammunition pouches carrying two charged magazines each. There were other pouches on the belt, but he didn't want to take the extra time to inspect it thoroughly. Instead, he passed the belt to Vicky and let her do it.

Goran's pockets yielded a treasure trove of useful items and information. The first item he collected was a Michelin Road map of the city of Mosul. A cursory glance showed him that Nineveh was clearly marked and that there were several pencil marks that would bear closer inspection. He refolded the map and stuffed it in his back pocket.

From her breast pocket he removed a bloodstained booklet that looked homemade.

Doing his best to keep the blood from getting all over his hands, he opened the booklet and found to his surprise and pleasure it was a Peshmerga C.E.O.I. (communications/electronics operating instructions). A C.E.O.I. is a kind of combat order, created for the technical control and coordination of communications inside a command.

Typically, they include current and up-to-date information covering radio call signs and frequencies, a telephone directory, code words for elementary encryption, passwords, authentication tables, and visual and sound signals. The bloody booklet, a tightly restricted secret, was a gold mine. Brad passed it to Vicky, whose eyes widened as she realized what it was.

He found several other items in the dead colonel's pockets, not the least of which was a small notebook filled with tiny Arabic script. Brad tucked that into his shirt pocket to give to Jessica as soon as he had time. He could read a little

Arabic, mostly common usage words like the ones on street signs; Jessica was the best on the team at reading the script.

The last item he dug out of her pockets was a small velvet bag containing an amulet, a small piece of pewter with a scissor-like double bladed scimitar terminating in two points stamped into it. He heard Pashew's gasp of shock when he removed the amulet from the pouch and he glanced up at her, curious to know what had precipitated her reaction.

"What?" Jessica asked. She had noticed Pashew's shocked expression and followed her gaze to the amulet in Brad's hand. "Let me see it…" She reached out her hand and Brad passed it to her as Pashew watched in horror.

Jessica squinted at the necklace and then took a tiny penlight from the pocket of her shirt. When the beam of light struck the amulet, it was Jessica's turn to gasp. Then her eyes hardened and she turned to Pashew.

"You knew?" she asked in Kurmanji.

A look of angry, though frightened, defiance swept over Pashew's face.

"You too?" Jessica asked, her face a mask of horror.

"What the hell is going on?" Brad asked anxiously. Jessica was usually unflappable, but her reaction to the amulet was interesting enough that he had to know the reason for it.

Jessica locked eyes with her cousin.

"This amulet!" she raged, her lips drawn back in a snarl. "This amulet is a Shi'ite talisman, a representation of Zulfiqar, the legendary sword of Ali ibn Abi Talib. The scimitar is said to have been given to him straight from the hand of Muhammad.

"Muhammad had received it from the hand of Jibraeel (Gabrial "Lord of Angels") when Allah commanded it." She turned her rage back on Pashew and held the amulet up in front of the woman's face. "You *bitch*... This is a DAESH charm!" she raved. "The people who murdered your husband and your child!"

Pashew blanched and then hissed in guttural sounding Kurmanji, "You speak of things you do not comprehend." Jessica backhanded her.

Ving reached up with one massive hand and stopped her, but Jessica continued her rant.

"She's one of them, Brad! She's a traitor to her people and to the memory of her own husband and child!" Jessica was sobbing, angry tears coursing down her cheeks.

*   *   *

Ving had tied Pashew's hands and feet with her own bootlaces and then pacified Jessica as best he could. He had taken Pashew's M-16 from her, ripping it roughly from her shoulder after he had thrown her and her mother into the van. Rather than leaving it within easy reach of Jessica, he handed it to the wounded Pete to secure before he began his own search of Pashew. The captain struggled to avoid his big hands, but Ving was ruthless. He was pissed, too, but not as pissed as Jessica had been.

His search of her person yielded little of any interest, though she had struggled mightily as he patted down the outside of her shirt around her breasts. Despite her resistance, he had reached inside her fatigue shirt to remove a small bundle of papers that appeared to be insignificant when he briefly glanced at them. He stuffed them inside his own shirt, intending to look more closely at them when he got a chance. When he was done, he rolled her over face down on the floor and forgot about her. And the papers.

*   *   *

Brad crawled over everyone to reach the passenger seat, but it had turned out to be hard as hell to read the Michelin map in the dim light cast by the dashboard lights, especially traveling fast down an unimproved road in a hard sprung vehicle. He tried borrowing Jessica's penlight and holding it in his teeth, but that didn't work because he was jouncing around so much that the tiny circle of light was constantly moving. Looking overhead, he searched for a dome light but there was none visible.

"It's back here," Vicky called out, pointing at the roof above her.

"Thanks," Brad answered as he moved back into the cargo compartment. He grunted from the effort of shoving Colonel Goran's body up against the back doors. "Her too!" he ordered, pointing at Pashew.

Anger and fear warred with each other on her face as Vicky roughly shoved her into a position next to Goran. No one had bothered to close Goran's eyes, they were dull and lifeless. Pashew found herself nose to nose with the corpse of her mother and unable to turn away.

Brad stood up and flicked the switch on the dome light then sat back down on the floor. The soles of the hiking boots he was wearing pressed against Pashew's buttocks, but he didn't care. He spread the Michelin map out on the floor and scrutinized it carefully.

There were pencil marks scattered over the city with Arabic names scribbled beside some of them. There were other marks that had nothing written beside them. Unable to decipher the scribbling, he motioned for Jessica to move over and help him. She moved away from Pete, who had wrapped the blue bandana around his thigh and tightened it to stanch the bleeding, and knelt beside Brad.

"No wonder you couldn't read this," she said thickly. She was still seething, and her lips were stretched tight across her teeth. "These are not common usage words, these are people's names." She read off several before her voice trailed off as the tip of her forefinger continued to move from scribble to scribble.

"Do you see Kavoosi's name on there?" Charlie asked.

Jessica flashed him a dirty look, but she kept on reading.

*   *   *

Brad sat back on his haunches, mentally conducting a reassessment of the situation. There was no one in the city that he could trust, even his own government was out to stop him. All of Mosul was engulfed in a violent conflict. Because of the similar uniforms, it would take a scorecard and a referee to recognize all the players, friendly, neutral, and otherwise.

U.S. troops, Canadians, French, German, Belgian, and even a handful of Swiss troops mixed in with Iraqi Special Forces, Infantry, and the Iraqi State police were fighting street to street with DAESH troops, and civilians were scattered freely among both sides. Tens of thousands of citizens who just wanted to get away from the bloodbath were fleeing in the streets, and they were often caught in the crossfire.

He stared down at the Michelin map, and then, with a red colored pencil he had grabbed from the glove compartment, he began to mark out the names Jessica had translated. After he finished doing that, he circled locations he himself would have fortified had he been conducting a combat operation in the city.

Moving over to sit beside Vicky, who was leaning back against the bare metal wall of the van with her eyes closed, Brad put his mouth close to her ear.

"No sign of pursuit yet, which is weird," he whispered. "We have to find a place to pull over and hide to see if they will mount one."

Vicky turned her head so that their lips were almost touching.

"We need to interrogate her," she whispered. "I don't like it, but she's holding out on us."

Brad glanced over at Pashew. "I don't like it, Vicky. I don't hold much with torture…"

"Even if it means Murphy dies?"

Brad had no comeback for that.

FOURTEEN

Back in the front passenger seat, Brad instructed Jared to slow down and began to search for a turnoff, someplace that would provide them concealment at the very least while they waited to see if there was any pursuit from the camp. He pointed to what appeared to be some kind of turnaround in a wooded area, and Jared turned off the van's lights and drove off the road into it.

Leaving Vicky fuming in the van with Pashew and Pete, the engine still running in case the pursuit showed up, Brad, Jared, Ving, Charlie and Jessica exited the vehicle and began a hasty three-hundred-sixty-degree reconnaissance of the surrounding area. When they returned, satisfied that there was no one near, Brad slipped inside the van and shut the engine off. Vicky started to speak, but Brad put his finger to his lips and stepped back outside.

The four of them listened silently, ears straining for any sound of racing engines, and they watched for lights from the edge of the roadway. There were no lights, and the only sounds were the ticking sound of the engine cooling and the sounds the night birds made flitting through the trees.

"Nothing." Jessica whispered.

"Then there's no reason to whisper, Jess," Brad said with a wry chuckle.

"This ain't right," Ving said, shaking his bald head. "They should have been after us like a bat out of Hell."

"Yeah, we have their commander," Jared agreed softly.

Brad pursed his lips, and it looked clear he was struggling with something. After a few short minutes he spoke.

"Perhaps they know something about the colonel we don't..."

Vicky stepped out the van's cargo door, dragging Pashew behind her. The captive couldn't walk, she could only hobble as Vicky shoved her to the edge of the cleared area closest to the road. Vicky had found a folding knife with a wicked looking blade in a pouch on Goran's web belt, which she was now wearing around her slim waist. She opened the blade and was holding it at Pashew's throat.

The fear in Besna Pashew's eyes was real. She had seen more beheadings and torture—including the stoning of her own child—than any human should have to, though she believed with all her heart that the atrocities had been necessary. Indeed, she believed that they had been mandated by the Prophet, blessed be his name, which was the same as if it had come from the lips of Allah himself.

The loss of her husband was of no import, she never loved him. Her father and mother had betrothed her to the older man when she became six years old and he disgusted her. It had been his fault that their daughter Keje had been stoned to death.

Besna glanced toward the back of the van, where her mother's corpse lay cooling slowly. Ester Goran had been as outraged as Besna herself at Keje's tragic and ignominious death, and the event had been the pivotal factor in their shift in allegiance to the Islamic State. Ester had already been an officer in the Peshmerga, and it was she who arranged for Besna's commissioning.

When Besna had finally been transferred into the PAK, they had worked together to undermine the organization as subtly as possible. If they had been discovered, they would have been executed immediately. She was going to miss her mother, but she intended to keep on fighting, and it was her duty to keep these perplexing infidels from jeopardizing Kavoosi or his group of ISIS warriors.

The really perverse, almost humorous, aspect of it all was that the order to protect Kavoosi at all costs had come from within the infidels' own government.

She was also puzzled; her imminent torture seemed more a tool of ISIL, not of the Americans she had seen and worked with. Americans appeared soft, they did not have the discipline, the hardness or the belly to do whatever was necessary to extract information from a prisoner.

Amongst the zealots of ISIL, being captured by the Americans was almost considered a vacation. American prisoners were fed, sheltered, and not subjected to the harsh treatment accorded to infidels by the tenets of the Jihad. These Americans were not like the others she had seen, especially this red-headed she-devil with the hard green eyes, and Besna was not yet ready to be martyred for the cause.

Besna steeled herself for what was to come, but there remained still another tactic she could employ that would permit her to continue to serve her cause. Sharia law said it was admissible to lie if the end goal was justified and that lying was actually an obligation if the end served the faith. Lying to one's enemies was not a sin. She would have to endure a bit of discomfort so that she did not give the appearance of deception or of making it too easy for them. She could, however, allow them to "pry" some information of no consequence from her lips.

Certainly a few of the faithful might die from her revelations, but the vitally important work of Hamid Kavoosi must not be hindered. The thought struck her like a thunderbolt. Kavoosi's group appeared much larger than the infidels', and they were armed and fanatically vigilant. Surely some of the faithful would die if she revealed the location where they were holding the prisoner, but they would die with the name of Allah on their lips and be instantly transported to Paradise.

Brad's eyes became drawn to the captain's deep brown eyes. He saw fear there plainly, but there was something more, something she was concealing. He caught Vicky's eye and made a motion indicating that she should put the knife away. Vicky looked confused, but she complied anyway.

"Ving, Jared, get the colonel and Stark out of the van. We're not taking them with us." His eyes never left Pashew's.

*   *   *

He stepped carefully over the rubble in the street, not as worried about taking care of his thousand dollar hand-lasted Italian shoes as he was about remaining undetected. Mosul's Old City had never been a safe place, but in the chaos of the struggle between ISIL and the allied forces for dominion over the headquarters of the Caliphate it felt doubly dangerous. There were patrols by the Golden Division, by the allied forces, by ISIL, and even by gangs of civilians searching for food and weapons running freely through the ruined streets.

Logic and common sense told him he must be insane to venture out into the hell of Mosul's Old City, especially down near the waterfront, but there was far too much at stake for him to pay much attention to them. Instead, he armed himself to the teeth and skulked in the shadows, avoiding contact with anyone, friend or foe. The meeting he had been summoned to was worth the risk.

The row of old homes along the ruined street had been reduced to crumbling piles of handmade brick and block. But he found the entrance to the dank cellar of the last home on the street and ducked into the relative safety of its welcoming blackness and held his breath, listening for any sound. The distant sounds of rifle fire reverberated in the night outside, but there was someone in the cellar with him, he could hear the sound of breathing.

"I was getting ready to give up on you," the familiar voice said from the recesses of the cellar. The smell of dried vegetables and spices permeated the clamminess of the room. The cellar had been used for storage for centuries, he knew. This was not his first meeting in this place, but if his luck held, it might be his last.

"Too damned many crazies out tonight," he muttered in response. He couldn't see the man he was talking to, but he didn't need to. They had known each other all their lives.

"Speaking of crazies," the man said, "Jacobs and his group are on the loose."

"How the hell did that happen?" he exploded.

"I don't know, but he managed to take both of your assets with him."

In a fit of temper he kicked the damp wall of the cellar. He knew it had to have badly scuffed his expensive shoes, and it really hurt his toes. The pain did nothing to assuage his temper.

"I don't have to tell you what's at risk here if Jacobs gets to Kavoosi," he said through gritted teeth. "It's not just the money. It's our *asses!*"

"Yeah. I don't even want to think about the billions of dollars, but I'm more concerned about keeping my skin intact." The man's voice sounded tense, and it was easy to tell from his tone he was angry. "I've got a sweet deal going here; I can make money another time … if I live through this cluster fuck. How the hell did Murphy manage to get himself caught anyway, Parker? Why was he even in Al-Tameem?" His tone was accusatory.

"He wasn't supposed to be. Apparently he got cut off, separated from the unit he was 'advising'. We had an asset in that unit, too, but he was killed earlier in the day."

The man heaved an exasperated sigh.

"So what are you going to do about this?"

Parker Willingham thought for a moment.

"You say he got Goran and Pashew both?"

"That's what I'm told."

"I have a dossier on Major Ghazi. We've been trying to approach her, but we've been damned careful about it. She's a real zealot."

"Whatever you do, you need to get it done quickly, Parker. If Jacobs gets to Murphy, he's going to kill Kavoosi, and you know what that means..."

"It means we are going to get our asses killed," Parker said bitterly.

"No," the man in the darkness said. "It means *you're* going to get *your* ass killed. If you don't get this fixed, and in one hell of a hurry, I'm cutting you loose... You'll be on your own."

"You can't mean that!"

"Oh, yes I can, and I can do it too. I have a fallback plan, I always do. Unfortunately for you, the fallback plan requires that I sacrifice something important to me—you."

*   *   *

"Brad, we can't just leave them here," Vicky said softly.

The turnaround they had stopped in sat on the edge of an olive grove, apparently where the harvest vehicles were parked during the harvest. He had been sitting with his back against the trunk of an ancient olive tree, thinking about what

Pashew had revealed to him. She was still holding something back, of that much he felt certain.

"Huh?" he asked as Vicky's voice jerked him back to real time.

"The bodies, Brad, we can't just leave them here."

He frowned. "We don't have shovels to bury them with, Vicky, but we sure as hell can't take them with us..."

"You just figure out what we're gonna do next, Brad," Jared said. "Me and Charlie and the Bacon Man here can scratch out a couple of shallow graves with the tire wrench and then cover them with some of these stones. He looked pointedly at several piles of stones adjacent to the turnaround, apparently stacked there by orchard workers.

"You're bein' awful free with my labor there, Smoot..." Ving joked, but he was already up and moving to the back of the van. It was an unpleasant task but one he knew needed to be done. The bodies were already out and on the ground. Goran's body lay on its back, sightless eyes staring up into the moonlit night. Vicky had closed Stark's eyes at some point before they stopped.

Ving open the rear doors and lifted the cover off the spare tire compartment. He let out a long, low whistle when he saw the C-4 packed around the tire and the gas tank beneath it.

"Did y'all know we were riding around on a damned bomb?" he asked, looking for the detonator. "It's set up to go off by remote. We need to find the remote or unload this shit before I'm gettin' back inside this thing..." He glanced over at Jared. "I nominate Smoot here for disposal duty if we can't find the remote... Just returnin' a favor you understand."

"Thanks a lot, Ving," Jared said dryly, "I 'preciate that."

"Brad has the remote guys..." Vicky said.

"Leave the C-4 guys. We're going to have to figure out a way to rearm ourselves, and having a ready-made bomb at hand may come in handy in Mosul."

Ving sighed. "I knew it, we're gonna end up walkin' before this is over, I can feel it!"

The soil appeared soft and rock filled, but Charlie and the two men made short work of scraping out two graves and were soon piling stones atop the corpses.

Brad continued to stare at the Michelin map, and when Ving and Jared were finished, he stood up.

"Jess," he called out, "how are you and Pete doing?"

"I can talk, Brad," Pete replied. "It's my leg that got hit, not my mouth. I'm fine, I can still walk. I've been hurt a lot worse than this and managed to keep going."

"You sure, buddy?"

"I'm good, brother. I was just waiting for those guys to finish digging before I said anything. Those damned stones looked awful heavy…"

FIFTEEN

"Here," Brad said, pointing at a spot on the map. "That's where we need to go. Jared nodded and put the van in gear then drove to the edge of the roadway. Both of them took another look down the road to see if there was any sign of pursuit, but there were no lights visible.

"That just plumb makes me nervous," Jared muttered.

Brad agreed with him, but he didn't say so. He was busy staring at the map, which he still had opened. The spot he had indicated to Jared on the map was on the north side of Mosul, on the Tigris River, just upstream from the ferry terminal. The closest route there, according to the marks Goran had made on the map and the information he had gotten out of Pashew, would skirt all the known hostile combatants and did not appear to have any logical places for friendlies to attempt to blockade.

Turning to the team, he glanced back at Pashew before deliberately speaking in English rather than Arabic.

"I marked the GPS coordinates for the gravesites on the map so the bodies can be recovered later. I couldn't care less if Goran is eaten by wild dogs, but Stark deserves better than an unmarked grave in this sand box."

He watched Pashew closely as he spoke, looking for any indication that she might understand what he was saying. There was none. Still unsatisfied, he gave Vicky a knowing look and then he spoke.

"Kill her."

Pashew gave no sign she knew what was coming until she saw the look of grim determination on Vicky's face as the redhead withdrew the knife from Goran's web belt and snapped it open with a flick of her wrist. When Vicky grabbed Pashew's hair none too gently and bent her head back, she gave the nasty looking blade an elaborate flourish before placing it beneath Pashew's chin, the tip pressing into the soft skin enough to draw blood.

Pashew's eyes fluttered in shock as she realized Vicky's intent. Only then was Brad satisfied that the woman did not understand English. But even so he decided to couch his words in subtle terms so that, if she had managed to fool him, she would not comprehend what he was saying when he outlined the plan that was still forming in his mind.

"Take her to the back of the van, Vicky, and blindfold her … and see if you can find something to plug her ears with."

Vicky felt a mild flash of irritation at being ordered around like a peon, but it passed quickly. There were only so many people in the team, and she was sitting closest to Pashew. Force Recon teams operated a little differently than what she was used to, and for the first time she realized that adjusting to the ways of Brad's team was going to be a little harder than she'd anticipated.

She did as she was ordered, shoving Pashew roughly up against the back doors, facing away from the team, and then blindfolded her with a bandana from her own hip pocket. As she tied the bandana, she made a mental note to acquire several more of the large bandanas to carry in the field. It was amazing how many uses she had found for them. Then she rummaged around in her pockets for something to use as ear plugs but came up empty.

A memory flitted through her mind, an image of Stark on their lone weekend fling. Stark had been leaning against a picnic table, his handsome profile outlined against the setting sun while the seabirds' lonesome cries echoed above, and he was lighting … a cigarette.

"Brad, could you check in the console and see if there's an ash tray?"

Brad turned to her.

"You thinking of taking up smoking?"

"No, but Paul smoked, and I need a couple of butts to use as ear plugs if there are any there..."

In short order, two half smoked cigarettes were passed back to her. She tore the remnants of paper and tobacco from the filters, and then wadded the filters up and stuffed them into Pashew's ears. One more check of the bandana for tightness and she was finished.

"We're going to the north side of Mosul. Up above the Terminal de Ferri the Tigris takes a sharp bend, and there's a road that parallels the river. We'll scout the riverbank until we find a small boat... If we can't find a fisherman's boat we'll move on foot down to the Al-Jazeera Recreational Park. The Michelin guide says they have boat rentals there."

He held up the map, though it was really too dim inside the van for any of them to read it. His forefinger pointed to a spot on the map.

"This is the Khosr River. It joins the Tigris just east of the old City of Nineveh, where the ruins of the Mosque of the Prophet Jonah, or Yunus as it is named in the Quran, are. Stark said that's where Murph is being held, and our guest here"—he nodded in the direction of Pashew—"not only confirmed it, she gave me a specific location in the ruins.

The Khosr runs underneath three bridges, the third of which is the Al-Suez Bridge, where we leave our boat and follow the broad boulevard straight down to the mosque. It's still going to be full dark when we get there, as long as we hustle."

"What are we gonna do if it takes too long to find a boat or if we get held up by hostiles or even by friendlies?" Ving asked.

"I was getting to that," Brad said with a grin. He tapped the holstered pistol on Vicky's web belt. "You may have noticed we are slightly under-armed for combat. All we have right now are this pistol and that M-16 Pete is sitting on."

"I wondered where that went," Jessica remarked and began feeling around on the floor around the wounded pilot.

"Hey!" Pete said in mock dismay. "Keep your hands to yourself, girl!"

"In any case," Brad said, ignoring the byplay, "we have to stop in one of the built-up areas and go shopping for weapons before we can even think about going in after Murph. According to the captain there, Kavoosi and his men are loaded for bear."

"We got a buttload of C-4 and a remote detonator too," Ving added.

"Yes we do, but I don't plan on carrying it down the riverbank in my hands, Ving. We need to pick up explosives when we get our other weapons." He hesitated for a moment. "I really don't want to rip off any friendlies … and, before you ask, if we get engaged by any friendlies we disengage at once. We defend ourselves, but we disengage *immediately*."

"That's gonna make our 'shopping' trip a little more difficult…"

"It is what it is, Jared. This is sticky enough without getting into it with friendlies."

"If we're not going to take the C-4," Ving said thoughtfully, "what are we going to do with her?" He stared pointedly at the tense figure at the back of the van. "I don't see us dragging her along with us. Pete's going to slow us down enough as it is, and we don't have to worry about him giving us up to the bad guys."

Pete laughed. "I can keep up, Bacon Man, but you're right, she's going to be a real problem."

"We can't kill her. I don't know if that major knows she's a turncoat or not, but I do know PAK is aware that we took her and the colonel from the camp…"

"The colonel is already dead, Brad," Vicky argued. She was not being bloodthirsty, she was being practical.

Brad made a command decision.

"We're roughly ten miles from Mosul. We leave her by the side of the road, still trussed up but without the blindfold. Vicky, when we leave, you toss her mother's knife out into the roadway, making sure she sees it. By the time she crawls over and cuts herself free we will be long gone."

No one raised any objections.

*   *   *

Finding a fishing dory turned out to be far easier than Brad expected. They had parked the van just before midnight local time in a field at the apex of the bend where the Tigris turns back south, about a thousand feet above the northern tip of the island designated as the Al-Jazeera Recreational Park. Either through what they figured to be sheer luck or as the result of a lazy fisherman's eagerness to return home, they located a twenty-foot dory pulled up on the south bank of the river.

At first glance, the boat seemed a godsend, but upon closer inspection, they discovered why the boat had been beached and left. The smell of rotting fish emanated from the center of the boat, shezboot and masgouf fish that sold in the city marketplaces for the equivalent of nearly four dollars each. The fish were dead and dry, and there was human blood on the front and rear seats.

An ancient, bullet-riddled Johnson outboard was tilted forward, though not locked in place, indicating that the boat had been hurriedly beached. The prow had been banged up, but once they pushed it out into the river, it did not seem to be leaking too badly. The outboard, totally useless, was jettisoned over the side, and two fence posts were hurriedly uprooted to be used as push poles or oars. In a matter of minutes, the team was poling the dory out into the swift waters of the Tigris.

The name Tigris is based on an Old Persian word, *"Tigra"*, which means "The fast one". The water is shallow and silt-filled, and the river-dwellers are more partial to shallow draft rafts or *kuphar* (round boats with flat bottoms) than boats. The current is so swift that it is difficult to navigate upstream, and the rafts are often discarded and permitted to float away downstream.

Using the fence posts proved awkward, but Ving managed to maneuver to the center of the river until they reached the Al-Jazeera Park. Brad indicated with a finger that Ving should take the east channel around the island, avoiding the possibility of prying eyes on the Park docks or the ferry terminal. They had a tense moment when the bottom of the dory scraped a sandbar as they passed back into the main stream, but it was quickly forgotten as the Al Shohada Bridge seemed to race towards them.

The night had turned partially cloudy, which helped them pass unnoticed beneath a second, larger bridge. There were armed men posted on the second bridge, but they were jabbering back and forth and did not notice the slender coracle.

The third bridge, known as "The Old Bridge", was an old type iron structure mounted on thick concrete pylons. There were no troops on the bridge, the entrance to Nineveh, because DAESH had mined and booby trapped it to keep the Iraqis and their allies from mounting an assault on the ancient city. Ving moved them close inshore on the west side of the river, tensing up each time the dory scraped the rocks covering the shallow bottom.

The last thousand feet or so before the junction of the Khosr River were fraught with anxiety in the stillness of the night. They all felt as if they were being watched, and all they had to defend themselves in the event they were detected were Pashew's M-16 and the Czech pistol, which would be useless against rifles on the bank of the river.

The entrance to the Khosr River almost slipped past them. Only Ving's massive upper body strength kept them from being swept past. All Jared could do with the other fence post was try to keep the prow from lodging against the exposed stones as the river grew progressively narrower. As they passed beneath the Old Bridge yet again, they all had to climb out and portage the boat over the spillway, which was not shown on the map.

None of them were able to breathe freely until they made it safely past the spillway and into the slower water beyond. The spillway was going to put a crimp in Brad's escape plan, but it seemed too late to worry about it, they were committed. The slower current made forward movement easier, but the narrower river and the proximity of buildings on either side necessitated a slower, stealthier pace. It was nerve wracking.

The Khosr flows through the center of ancient Nineveh and into the ruins of the ancient city, but they only had to pass underneath two bridges to reach their debarkation point. They left the boat on the marshy bank of the Khosr, beneath the Al-Suez, the second bridge, and then crept through the darkness up into a greensward on the west side of the broad six-lane avenue that led to the Temple of the Prophet Jonah.

All of them except Jessica were surprised at the buildings around the boulevard, they had expected Nineveh to be a pile of ruins instead of a modern metropolis, though many of the buildings were in fact reduced to rubble from the recent fighting. The devastation was truly amazing. The old city, the ruins, was north of the Khosr.

If it had not been for the war damage and the power being out, they would have been spotted long before they reached the Al-Suez Bridge. The realization sent chills up and down Brad's spine. Then he wondered what else he had assumed that might end up getting them killed.

He waved the team towards a modern three-story building that looked as if it had been hit by a tornado and pumped his fist in the air to signal the urgency of his command. They were exposed, and his combat senses were screaming danger. They barely made it inside the wreckage of the building before a motorized ISIS patrol rumbled across the Al-Suez Bridge and past the greensward they had just vacated.

The vehicles were pickup trucks with makeshift armor plate welded around the driver and around the machine gun pedestals in the beds. The trucks were painted a flat black, and they were loaded with rifle toting black clad lunatics. The team watched as the trucks surrounded a small group of fleeing civilians trying to cross the boulevard at a major intersection. They came to a halt and though it was difficult to see in the darkness, the team could make out the troops hopping off the trucks. There was a sound of screaming and suddenly a spate of shots rang out.

Ving growled deep in his chest, and Brad had to forcibly restrain him from running out into the street.

"Jesus, Brad, they're shooting kids!"

"And by the time you can get there, Ving, they'll all be dead and you will be the only target they have left to shoot at!"

Ving was trembling and near tears, and Jessica was crying as she looked at Brad imploringly.

273

"Isn't there anything we can do, Brad?"

He felt like a heel, but the situation was impossible. They were helpless to do anything to save the civilians. They needed weapons, and they needed them fast. He looked for the highest vantage point he could reach in the ravaged building and then caught Jared's attention with a hand signal.

Pointing to the high spot and using his forefinger and middle fingers, he aimed them first at his eyes then the trucks. Jared, who had the best eyesight, day or night, of the team, nodded and began the climb.

SIXTEEN

Their weapons and ordnance had all been confiscated back at the PAK tent city. All they carried for weapons were the Czech CZ 75 9mm pistol they had taken from Goran's body and the M-16 Jessica had taken from Pashew.

Brad motioned to Vicky to hand over the pistol, but when she tried to take it out of the holster, he signaled impatiently for her to hand over belt, holster and pistol together.

"You're not going this time, Vicky."

She started to protest, but her mouth snapped shut. His reasoning was sound. She hated the idea of being left behind, but she realized that he wasn't trying to protect her. There were only two weapons available to them at the moment. Jared was carrying the M-16, which seemed the obvious choice because he was the best marksman of the team.

Vicky forced herself to think like Brad. He was going to go out to steal more weapons, and unarmed team members would be a liability that he could not afford. She looked up at the clearing night sky and tried to estimate how much longer the darkness might last. When daylight came, negotiating the city would be impossible to accomplish without being detected. At best, they had about three hours left before daybreak.

They were going to need to find a good place to hole up during the daylight hours because there was no way Brad and Jared were going to be able to rearm the team in three short hours. It was frustrating because they had no way of knowing whether the PAK major had alerted the other friendlies or even if she was a turncoat, too, and had alerted DAESH. Time was getting short for Brandon Murphy either way, providing he wasn't dead already.

*   *   *

Jared lay on a shattered section of third-story floor that jutted out towards the boulevard. He crawled out as far as he dared until he felt the concrete shift beneath his weight. Carefully he stretched out in the prone position and focused on the small circle of trucks. His night vision was exceptional, and he could make out the DAESH bastards as they kicked at the bodies of the civilians they had murdered.

There was a small group collected to one side of the last truck, from their size and clothing Jared assumed they were young women. His gut churned as he thought about what was in store for them. The intel reports he had read stated bluntly that DAESH regularly took females, the younger the better, and used them as sex slaves. Forcing his mind away from his fury, he concentrated on the apparent leader of the group. He was waving his arms, obviously giving orders for their next move.

The troops loaded back onto the trucks, leaving three men to take control of the females. The commander waved in the direction of a storefront on the west side of the intersection, and the three men herded their captives toward it while the trucks started up and moved westward down a side street. The building the captives were taken to appeared to be pretty well intact, though the windows and door glass had been blown out.

When the sound of the trucks died out, Jared waited a few moments to see if there would be any movement around the bodies. There was no movement at all on the vast thoroughfare ... anyone who had been near obviously heard the screams and gunshots and vacated the area. Jared slowly climbed back down to the rest of the team.

*   *   *

"We have three guys and a handful of kids in that three-story building on the corner, Brad."

"Girls I bet," Vicky said bitterly. Jared could only nod, and Jessica's face became a mask of rage.

"Could you see well enough to tell if they carried anything bigger than small arms?" Brad's tone was hopeful.

"Too far away."

"We'll have to take what we can get and be grateful for that." He paused for a moment. "Guess we'd better get moving." He reached for the pouch on the web belt and took out Goran's knife, handing it to Vicky. "I hate leaving you with nothing more than this to defend yourselves." He turned to Charlie and Jessica. "You two still have Jared's knives?"

"Yeah, we still have them, Brad. We're ready to go."

"Not this trip, Charlie. I'm taking Jared and Ving. I want the rest of you to stay here and keep utterly silent."

None of them looked happy about being left behind, but Brad's statement had been a command, not a request, and they knew it. They also knew that Ving was the deadliest man with his hands that any of them had ever known, and he was as strong as a mule if Brad lucked out and needed to carry back a buttload of weapons or ordnance.

*   *   *

They exited their hideout through what remained of the rear, scrambling over debris and around piles of rubble. There was an alleyway behind it that ran southwards toward the building Jared had identified. The alleyway appeared strewn with rubble and damaged vehicles.

Moving quietly was a bitch, but the three of them were masters of their craft, and anyone standing anywhere close to the alley would never have heard their passing. Evenly spaced, they kept a distance of about four meters between them. The biggest danger was being spotted.

Most people never learn to use their night vision well, especially city dwellers. Soldiers and Marines are taught that motion is the easiest method of detecting the presence of personnel in the darkness. Untrained troops tend to stare too long at one spot at night, straining to see clearly. When that happens, the eyes begin to play tricks, and shadows come to life.

The proper technique, one that has to be learned, practiced, and refined over years, is to keep the eyes constantly moving, never remaining in one spot for too long. Properly executed, even a person with poor night vision can detect motion. Brad, Jared and Ving possessed fantastic night vision, but Jared's was best of the three. He led the way, point man for the tiny patrol.

A soft clang of metal against metal sounded in front of them, and Jared raised his left fist instinctively, taking a knee behind the burned out hulk of a small Toyota pickup truck. He turned his head to see if

Brad and Ving had seen his signal, but they were both already down on one knee. Years of training and experience working together in every kind of weather and terrain made their movement to contact a textbook example of proper and effective technique. Noise and light discipline, the understanding and usage of hand signals, night vision techniques, and boldness tempered with caution combined with the shared bond of combat rendered them almost invisible—and highly efficient. In effect, they became ghosts.

Jared's eyes picked out motion ahead of them. The tension in his body eased as he watched a stray cat nosing an empty can out into the ally, trying to get its too large head into the open top to get at some tiny morsel of the can's contents. Stray cats were ubiquitous in the streets of Mosul, but dogs were a rarity. In Iraq, as in most of the Islamic world, dogs are generally deemed basically and ritually unclean. Even dogs kept as pets or working animals, they generally usually stay outdoors instead of in the home. Because of that and a common bias against spaying or neutering dogs, the population of feral dogs has become an uncontrollable nuisance.

Iraqis generally view the dogs as a pest at best and a threat to public safety at worst. Among the general populace, rumors and stories of deadly attacks by packs of dogs, dingoes and coyotes at night are common. Baghdad's provincial government declared in 2008 that thirteen people had been killed by wild dogs. Saddam Hussein instituted regular dog hunts in order to pacify residents, and the practice had extended to Mosul. After he became deposed, the practice had actually expanded. Few dogs roamed the streets of Mosul.

The three men rose as one and continued down the alleyway, halting at every sound. Patience was their watchword. A single mistake could get them all killed. Twice they had to scurry for cover when a roving patrol, another of the black pickup trucks, passed by on the next street over. It took them over an hour to get to the rear of the building that held the captive girls.

Brad took up a position at the rear corner of the building and Ving knelt by the wall next to the steel back door. Jared crept, silent as a shadow, along the damaged north wall of the building. It was a risk, his being exposed to the street side of the structure, but it was one that had to be taken.

Fortunately, the cloud cover had thickened, and Jared was able to peer through a three-foot breach in the outer wall about five feet off the ground. The opening was probably caused by an RPG (Rocket Propelled Grenade) or a LAW (Light Anti Armor Weapon) discarded by the Iraqi Army when DAESH had first begun to establish the Caliphate.

The girls were huddled inside against the south wall amidst the wreckage of office furniture. Several desks and chairs had been arranged in a rough semicircle around them. One of the men was posted next to the open front door, and another was posted at the rear of the large open room. Both were grinning lewdly at the group of frightened girls and not paying any attention at all to their duties, obviously feeling secure inside the ruined building.

The third man, obviously the leader, was leaning back in a swivel desk chair, stroking his beard and taunting the girls in Arabic. Jared felt the rage building inside of him, but he kept it bottled up because he knew the girls needed him to. There was no time to waste. He shrank back away from the hole in the wall and stole back to Brad as quickly as stealth would allow.

He motioned for Brad and Ving to follow him and they retreated across the alleyway and crouched in the lee of a retaining wall.

"There are still only three guards; back wall by the door, just inside the front door, and one in the center leering at the girls," Jared whispered without a trace of the rage he was feeling.

"Do they look alert?"

"Nope. Lecherous bastards are all leering at the girls."

"We're going to have to figure out a way to do this all at once, guys, we're only going to get one chance," Brad murmured.

Ving chuckled quietly. "Easy as pie, Brad. I'll take the back door, you guys take the back and the side."

"That ain't gonna work, Ving," Jared said. "I listened through a hole in the north wall, but if I miss or if the round passes through the asshole sitting on the girls, there's a good chance I could hit one of them."

"You ain't gonna miss, Jared; you're the best sniper I ever worked with."

"I've never test fired this weapon, Ving, I haven't sighted it in."

"So I'll take the back door and you and Brad here take the front at the same time."

"That might work," Brad said, "but how are you going to take down that armed man? Hell, you don't even know if that door is locked, he could shoot you right through the door…"

"Simple, Brad. We move on a fifty count. I take the back, you and Jared go to the front. On fifty, I knock on the door three times like I know what I'm doin'. The guy at the back has to check to see who's outside, and the other two are going to be distracted, either by me knockin' or those poor little girls. When the guy at the back opens the door, I'm gonna snatch that rifle right outta his hands and butt stroke his ass. You shoot the guy by the door with that pitiful little Czech pistol and Deadeye here shoots the guy in the middle. Game over."

The sheer audacity of the idea left Brad and Jared speechless for a moment.

"Better make it a hundred count. We have to be really quiet moving to the front, the windows are out and so is the door. Noise is going to carry in the night."

"You think we can carry this off, Brad?" Jared asked.

"It's all we've got, Jared, and we're running out of time. Did you see what kind of weapons they were carrying?" Jared shook his head no. Brad shrugged. "Let's do it." He began the count aloud at the Marine Corps marching cadence, a hundred and twenty beats per minute, so that the others would be in synch. Then the three of them moved out, as noiseless as the clouds moving above.

Brad and Jared high crawled past the blown out front windows to a position just shy of the blown out front door. The DAESH troops kept talking audibly inside in casual tones, and at the count of one hundred they could clearly hear the firm knocks made by Ving's ham-sized fists. The voices inside stopped, and then they heard a chuckle as the leader spoke in Arabic.

"Open it! Maybe the sergeant has sent us a gift of coffee and dates!"

Brad heard the sound of a big door bolt being drawn back and then there was a loud crash and a muffled yell. He threw himself through the door, landing on his back on the industrial high traffic carpet with the Czech pistol in both hands, pointed at the DAESH soldier. He pulled the trigger twice as fast as he could manage. Simultaneously, Jared stood in the doorway and fired two shots offhand into the startled face of the leader. Just that quickly, it was over.

Jared rushed over towards the girls to reassure them, but Brad stayed by the doorway, checking the man he had shot for any sign of a pulse and listening for the sound of vehicles. He heard nothing except the whimpering of the girls. The guard was DRT (Dead Right There).

The door guard was a real cowboy. He was carrying only a CAR-4, but his web belt had four magazine pouches hanging from it, and all were full of thirty-round magazines. A real prize hung from the side of the belt in a heavy leather scabbard. It was a small Kabjawal kukri, normally carried by British Gurkha soldiers in Iraq. The razor sharp knife had a wooden handle contoured for the hand.

The heavy leather sheath contained two pockets on the back, one of which held a small utility knife called a "karda", and the second pocket held a sharpener, called a "chakmak" for sharpening the blades or for striking sparks from flint. There was a notch, called a "kaura", in the blade by the hilt that served as a blood groove. It was in nearly new condition and had to have been taken from the body of a fallen Ghurka soldier or stolen, which was not as likely. Ghurkas are known for their fighting ability, and a prize such as this would not have been carelessly left lying about.

Jared was still trying, with little success, to calm the girls down. Ving had dragged the guard from the back door to the center of the room. The man was senseless and bleeding heavily from his mouth and nose. His head made a dull thud on the carpeted floor when Ving let go of him and bent down to search the body of the leader, whose face was mostly gone. He let out a low whistle.

"Bingo!" he said. He bent down and lifted a SAW (Squad Assault Weapon) from the floor beside the leader's body.

The SAW fired a 5.56 round, the same as an M-16 or CAR-4, and it was capable of firing linked ammunition or being fed by a banana-shaped thirty-round-capacity STANAG magazine, the same used for M-16s and CAR-4s. Treasure. The leader was also carrying a canvas bag with a couple of bandoliers of linked 5.56 ammo and several of the STANAG magazines.

Brad's attention was diverted from the unexpected wealth by a small cry from the girls and the sight of several of them running past him and out through the front door. Jared was running after them.

"Let 'em go, Jared," Brad said quietly. Jared stopped dead in his tracks and stared unbelievingly at him. "We can't help them, brother. There is no safe place for them, and they have dead parents out there they have to take care of. It's a religious thing with them, you know that."

Jared knew he was right, but he felt dejected. He had seen the ravages of war on several continents, and while he was almost immune to the savagery men inflicted on each other, he still had a soft spot for the kids who had to suffer even though they had done no wrong. Their misery was heartbreaking.

"Come on, buddy, we've got to grab the equipment these guys were toting."

"Yeah," Ving said, "and we need to get the hell outta here. No telling when their buddies are gonna come back for 'em."

"What are we gonna do with him?" Jared jerked a thumb at the lone living jihadist.

"Leave him," Brad said brusquely. "He's not going to be talking any time soon. You really did a number on his face, Ving..."

SEVENTEEN

The trip back to the rest of the team was almost as slow as the trip down to the office building. Before they reached the spot where Jared had encountered the stray cat, the bodies of the slain soldiers had apparently been discovered. Loud, angry shouts echoed off the walls of the buildings, and the flat black pickup trucks were swarming over the area. At one point they had been forced to hide in a large trash dumpster to avoid detection. The three men were breathing heavily when they finally reached the building with the rest of the team in it.

"Wow, you guys stink," Jessica remarked, pinching her nostrils shut.

"Yeah, we had to take our lunch break in a dumpster," Ving said, sniffing at his shirt.

"Never mind that," Vicky said impatiently. "All hell is breaking loose outside. In the last few minutes I must have seen a dozen of those black trucks go by. What happened?"

"No time for that now, Vicky. We need to get someplace a little more secure. It won't be long before they figure out we were on foot and they'll start a building to building search."

"Not a problem, Brad," Charlie called out. "While you guys were out for your little stroll, I did some exploring." He motioned for Brad to follow him, and Brad set his liberated bounty on the floor and complied.

"I don't really know what kind of place this was before it got clobbered," Charlie said, "but the owner liked his privacy." Pausing before an unusually wide door that appeared to lead to a janitor's closet, he twisted the door handle and opened it. There were mops, brooms, buckets, and cleaning materials inside, just as Brad expected, but they were all shoved to one side of the closet. Instead of stepping inside, Charlie bent over and lifted a corner of the carpet. The carpet was glued to a heavy wooden trapdoor, and when it came up it revealed a staircase leading down into a cool, dry cellar.

"Come on, you need to see this." Charlie led the way down into inky blackness and then switched on the penlight he had gotten from Jessica. The tiny circle of light swung around, illuminating a comfortably furnished office, with a desk, a few chairs, a long, narrow conference table, and an ancient Diebold safe with its door standing open as if it had been emptied in a hurry.

Brad heard the sound of a match striking and turned to see Charlie lighting a fairly new kerosene lamp.

"It's big enough for all of us, Brad, but there's no bathroom and no water, but there's a couple of cases of Coca Cola over in the corner."

Brad shook his head in disbelief then he clapped Charlie on the shoulder.

"That doesn't matter. There are plenty of buckets and disinfectants up in that closet. We'll make do. Right now we need to get everybody and all the gear down here as quick as we can." He raced up the stairs, Charlie close behind him.

They found a half empty two-gallon drum of kerosene in the closet at the top of the staircase along with three large, metal pails and assorted cleaning chemicals and disinfectants. A surprising number of the products bore familiar American names. There had also been two more kerosene lanterns on a bookshelf on the far side of the conference table.

Brad ushered everyone into the cellar and Ving shut the heavy trap door from the staircase. The building's owner had been clever about concealing the door. When it was shut from beneath, the glued down carpet concealed the door completely. If it had not been left open, Charlie would never have found it.

They were sitting on old, steel folding chairs around the conference table, taking inventory of the captured equipment. The M-249, the CAR-4, and three M-16s were lying in the center, and four U.S. Army issue web belts lay beside them. Vicky had taken the canvas bag that Brad brought back and emptied it out onto the table top. There were thirty STANAG magazines stacked on the table, seventeen of them fully charged with 5.56 military ball ammo. Two O.D. green cloth bandoliers of linked 5.56 ammo sat next to the magazines.

Goran's Czech CZ 75 9mm and its magazines were lying next to a Beretta 92F and three magazines. The rifles and the SAW were side by side, and Ving was checking each of them over carefully.

Jared was closely inspecting the Kabjawal kukri and its scabbard, hefting the razor shard blade in his hand and admiring its balance and workmanship.

"I'm keeping this baby," he said, sighting down the keen edge, which he aimed at a kerosene lamp's chimney glass. His own beloved Arkansas Toothpick, which he had carried for a dozen years, had been confiscated back at the PAK camp.

"And this baby is *mine,*" Ving stated emphatically, a broad smile creasing his jet-black face. He was cradling the machine gun in his hands as if it was an old friend. He reached down and snagged one of the charged magazines, inserted it into the weapons magazine well until it clicked, and then tapped it once to ensure that it was seated properly. Then he drew back the charging handle and jacked a round into the chamber before engaging the safety.

Brad performed the same ritual with the CAR-4 and then spoke to the others.

"You can divvy the rest of it up amongst yourselves. We still need one more rifle, but beggars can't be choosers." He had full confidence in the abilities of the other members of the team, and he didn't want any resentment or doubt to arise over who got what. Even the best of warriors could get aggravated over perceived slights under the pressures of combat.

Vicky solved the problem, reaching for Goran's web belt and the Czech pistol.

"Jared needs a rifle more than I do." Brad gave her a warm smile, which she returned.

Ving was shaking his head sadly.

"Does anybody else see what I see?" he asked, waving one massive hand across the table.

Brad nodded grimly, but Jessica and Charlie looked a little confused.

"It's all G.I. stuff," Pete said.

"It's like we gave them a damned military department store," Ving uttered in disgust. "And it didn't cost them one red cent."

DAESH had taken the City of Mosul as well as a lot more territory in June of 2014. And the Iraqi Army abandoned billions of dollars' worth of buildings, vehicles, weapons, and munitions that the U.S. Government gifted them when U.S. troops were drawn down. DAESH had promptly and gleefully appropriated all of it and were currently using it against the army that abandoned it, the American troops, and the allies.

Jared reached for the web belt that bore the scabbard for the kukri and began to adjust it to fit his waist. Then, surprising everyone, he reached for the Beretta, taking the holster and magazine pouch from their original belt and adding them to the one he had picked already.

"I reckon there's nearly two hours of dark left," he drawled. He reached down and pulled a kaffiyeh and an agal (a black circlet of rope that was used to secure the kaffiyeh) from the cargo pocket on the thigh of his jeans then removed his beloved Stetson from his head and donned the kaffiyeh. Then he placed the agal atop the cloth scarf.

"Jared, it's probably crawling with hostiles out there right now, hell, there's probably friendlies out there, too, by now—"

"It's still dark, Brad, and I'm wearing this rag on my head. I don't aim to let any of 'em get sight of me, but if they do, I'll look just like one of them in the dark. I ain't takin' the rifle with me, don't want to look like a threat to anybody. Besides, I caught a glimpse of something back by that damned smelly dumpster and I want to check it out... Could be exactly what I'm looking for."

*   *   *

Jared stole down the alleyway once again, even more silent than he had been the first time. He was in the zone, feeling it in the pit of his stomach and coursing through his body like an electric current. He had not been exactly truthful with Brad; he had seen something back down the alley, but it had not been by the dumpster. It had been nagging at him since before the ambush, something that triggered a memory long buried in his subconscious. It was the kukri's scabbard that triggered the memory, but when they returned to their hideout and entered the cellar Jared discovered that the memory had blossomed into his active memory.

In February of 2003, he had just been promoted to corporal after his graduation from Marine Corps SSBC (Scout Sniper Basic Course) at Quantico, Virginia and redeployed with his unit to Baghdad. On his arrival at the replacement detachment in-country, he had been assigned to his battalion's STA (Surveillance and Target Acquisition) Platoon.

In April of 2003, he and his partner had been on an intelligence mission trying to link up with a partisan offshoot of the Peshmerga that the Battalion S-2 wanted to coordinate with. The partisans had been reluctant to expose their identities to the rapidly dwindling but still powerful supporters of Saddam Hussein. Jared managed to affect the link-up with a man named Kevi Nahai, who was captain of one company of the partisan battalion.

Nahai had taken an immediate liking to Jared and his partner. He had taken them to his home to share a dinner meal of spicy lamb stew and *khubz* served with a hot black tea drink that Jared couldn't remember the name of. Jared noticed an odd mark carved on the door frame of the simple block house where Nahai lived. The symbol was a monochromatic line drawing of the blazing golden sun emblem (Roj in Kurdish) at the center of the flag of Kurdistan. The emblem's sun disk displayed twenty-one rays of equal size and shape with the exception of a single odd ray at the top and two even rays at the bottom. The number twenty-one is revered by the Kurds, representing the rebirth of the ancient native Kurdish religion of Yazdanism.

Over the course of the evening, Jared and Nahai had come to an agreement and had developed considerable respect for each other. Before Jared and his partner left, Nahai explained that the sign was actually the battalion's symbol. One of Jared's standout memories of the evening came when Nahai got ready to escort them to the outskirts of the neighborhood, where members of his company patrolled in the darkness to keep out the militant Hussein supporters.

Nahai moved aside a carpet bearing a pattern of peacock feathers hanging on the bare block wall of his home. Jared did not understand the significance of the feathers, but the carpet was obviously important to Nahai. The carpet concealed a recess with a false cover designed to look like the surrounding block. It was so cleverly executed that Jared did not see the outline of the cover at first. When Nahai opened the recess, a cache of startlingly expensive weaponry was revealed.

Nahai did not explain how he could afford the weapons, but one of the guns Jared saw was a Weatherby Magnum rifle with a Leupold scope. Nahai hesitated before taking out a Chinese copy of an AK-47, probably realizing that he may have just given away a secret that could endanger his family if it were leaked. Jared caught on to Nahai's expression of apprehension immediately and reassured him once more that they were on the same side and that his secret was safe. The doubt was plain on the Kurd's face, but he apparently resolved it to his own satisfaction and closed his 'safe' and replaced the carpet over it.

Over the course of the next eleven months, Jared became close to Kevi Nahai and his family. The two men learned to trust each other. It was a brotherhood born of combat, a lasting bond. When Jared returned for his next deployment, he visited the Nahai home, but it was in ruins. None of the neighbors seemed to know where he had gone. The only information he managed to garner was that Nahai's wife and daughter had been killed in the blast that destroyed their home.

The same sun symbol had been carved into the leather of the kukri scabbard, and that was what triggered the memory. That and the fact that Jared had seen the same symbol scratched on the door of one of the buildings near the dumpster in the alleyway they had hidden inside. Jared was moving back along the alleyway in the hopes of finding a member of the battalion and perhaps at least getting some useful information or, at most, another rifle. He realized that he was grasping at straws, but time was running out for Brandon Murphy and the team. Their little 'raid' had stirred up both DAESH and the friendlies, and vehicles were buzzing up and down the streets, and the sound of gunfire reverberated through the city.

He found the door he was looking for and slipped into the shadows to one side of it in case the residents were armed. It was taking a chance, but he felt compelled to take it. Opening the flap on the covered holster on his hip, he grasped the butt of the Beretta in case his wild-ass gamble turned to shit, and knocked on the door.

The door opened just a few inches, and Jared could see the startled, thinly bearded face of a young man of about seventeen. The young man's next words shocked him to the core.

"Agha Jared? Is that you?" The young man, excited, turned and shouted into the interior of the dwelling. "Father! Come quick! Agha Jared has come!"

*   *   *

Just before the first rays of the sun fell on Mosul, a battered old brown Datsun pickup with a homemade flatbed pulled up in the alleyway behind the building where the team was hiding. A canvas tarp covered the bed. As the truck brakes squealed and brought the vehicle to a gradual stop, there was movement under the tarp and Jared climbed out from beneath it carrying a large duffel bag.

No words were exchanged; everything that needed to be said had been said in Kevi Nahai's apartment. The moment Jared's weight came off the truck bed, there came the sound of grinding gears and the truck eased out of the alley and onto the street, moving slowly so as not to attract undue attention. Jared was inside the door and out of sight before the truck had completed the turn.

*   *   *

"Looks like you found what you were looking for," Brad remarked as Jared walked down the stairs with the duffel bag over his shoulder. With his kaffiyeh pulled around his face to hide his features, he looked like some weird Arab/cowboy Santa Claus.

"I found more than I expected, Brad, much more." Jared frowned. "Do you remember me telling you about Kevi Nahai?"

"The guy who lost his wife and daughter in Baghdad?"

"Yeah, and when I went back to see him when I redeployed, he was gone and no one could tell me where he went."

"Yeah, I remember you telling me about it."

"Well, he came here to Mosul ... and he lives down the alley near that dumpster where we had to hide!"

"That's wild! How did you figure that out?"

Jared lifted the scabbard on his web belt, showing Brad the emblem tooled into the leather.

"This is the emblem of Nahai's old unit in Baghdad. I had nearly forgotten about it until I saw it on this scabbard and then I noticed it carved on a doorpost in the alley. When I knocked on the door, Nahai's son Ferhad recognized me. I didn't know who he was at first; the last time I saw him he was around eight years old."

Vicky, who had come up to join them, spoke up.

"That's incredible."

"What's really incredible is what he gave me, Vicky," Jared said, walking over to the conference table and setting the duffel bag on top of it. The bag was marked "U.S.", but the stencil had been painted over. Jared unhooked the top and lifted out a Weatherby Mark V in .460 Magnum broken down into three pieces. He assembled it swiftly and confidently and then lifted it to his shoulder in an offhand firing position, the leather sling wrapped around his bicep and forearm.

"Jesus, I wish I had time to sight this in..." He worked the bolt, its nine locking lugs barely making a sound as they locked into place. "I'll have to use the iron sights. Kevi has the scope bore-sighted and zeroed at two hundred and fifty meters, but I don't remember his corrections and I forgot to ask him..."

"I hate to sound stupid, Jared, but what do you mean by 'corrections'?" Jessica asked.

Jared's eye never left the scope.

"Because of facial structure, the width and breadth of the cheekbones, the placement of the eyes on the face, everyone's view through the sights is slightly different, closer or further, higher or lower. The technical term is sight relief, and it refers to the distance between the eye and the sight aperture. Each individual has to make corrections, or adjustments, with the sight mechanism so that a weapon will strike exactly where the shooter aims. On an M-16, my corrections are three clicks to the left on the rear sight, and one click down on the front sight. I have no idea what it would be on this beast."

"Won't that make it hard for you to hit what you're shooting at?" she asked him.

"It would if we were out in the desert. Inside the city I'm not going to have to make many shots of two hundred yards or more."

"Bet that thing kicks like a mule," Ving observed.

"It does. It fires a 300-grain bullet at 3,100 feet per second, three times as fast as you can work the bolt, and each shot generates approximately a hundred foot pounds of energy in recoil."

"Must have a serious drop," Charlie said.

"Less than ten inches at two hundred yards. Not too bad, considering. For holdover I just aim at the chin and it will strike in the chest area at that range. Doesn't matter much. A hit anywhere on the body and your target is going down."

Pete grunted.

"Good squirrel gun."

Everyone chuckled except Jessica, who looked confused.

"You just shoot the tree and the squirrel gets vibrated to death," Brad explained. It was an old sniper joke.

"What else did you get from your old buddy, Jared?"

"You're going to like this, Ving," Jared replied, laying the impressive rifle down on the table and rummaging through the duffel. He set four boxes of cartridges for the rifle down on the table and then lifted out a half dozen black cardboard tubes about the size of a sixteen-ounce beer can. On the outside of each in white block lettering was the legend, "Grenade, Hand, Frag, M-67."

"Oh man!" Ving answered, reaching out to lift one of the containers from the table. Brad said nothing but let out a low whistle.

"Pay dirt!" Pete exclaimed.

"Tell me you got some C-4 and some detonators in there, boy!" Ving said hopefully.

"No C-4."

Ving's face dropped in disappointment.

"Unless you take these apart and get some from them..." Jared pulled four canvas bags from the bottom of the duffel. No one had to ask what those were. The M-18A1 claymore bag is as distinctive as the mine itself was. When the claymore is detonated, the explosion drives a matrix forward at a velocity of about 3,900 feet per second. At the same time the matrix breaks up into ball-shaped individual fragments. The balls are scattered in a fan-shaped pattern that is nearly six feet high and fifty-five yards wide at a range of about fifty yards.

The force of the detonation distorts the fairly soft steel fragments into a shape resembling a .22 caliber rimfire bullet. The fragments are effective out to a range of about a hundred yards, though they can travel out as far as two hundred and seventy yards. The result of the explosion is devastating. The bags also carried wire, a "clacker" (detonating device), and a tester. There was silence in the cellar for a moment, the only sound being the hissing of the kerosene lanterns. Jared had indeed struck gold.

EIGHTEEN

"This is the layout Kevi drew for me," Jared explained after he had withdrawn a folded square of sack paper from the inside of his shirt. He unfolded the paper and Brad weighted down three of the corners with the kerosene lanterns. Ving had laid one of the empty STANAG magazines on the fourth corner and was leaning forward on his elbows to get a closer look at the rough drawing.

Vicky stood behind Brad, saying nothing but listening closely to the conversation. Charlie and Jessica made Pete as comfortable as possible after cleaning and inspecting his thigh wound and then lay down for a nap. Brad had informed them that they would not be leaving their cellar until well after dark, and that was many long hours away. Pete, slightly embarrassed, had dry swallowed two Midol capsules from Jessica's fanny pack for the pain. They worked, and he was snoring softly.

The sketch was of the remains of the Mosque of the Prophet Yunus, who was referred to in the Christian Old Testament as "Jonah". It was located on top of a hill in eastern Mosul named Nebi Yunus, one of two mounds that formed a part of the ancient Assyrian city of Nineveh.

"DAESH blew up this mosque."

"Why the hell would they blow up a mosque?" Ving asked skeptically.

"Kevi said it was because the mosque was supposedly built over Jonah's tomb," Jared continued. "DAESH considered it to be a shrine, and, according to their way of thinking, the worshipping of shrines was not in keeping with their Islamic traditions."

Jared moved his forefinger to one side of the sketch, tracing a road that ran from the wide boulevard up around to the top of the hill the mosque had been built on.

"Mostly, this whole thing is just a monumental pile of rubble, but up here at the top there is a block of cell-like rooms connected by a sort of stone canopy supported by arched supports. That's where Kevi says they are holding Murph."

Brad's chin rested on his palm, his elbow supported by the conference table.

"Did he have any troop estimates or how they were armed?"

"He says there are thirty of them plus their leader, Kavoosi. They seem to work three shifts, ten men to a shift. He also said the bastards have dug tunnels under the rubble, and that they made a pretty exciting discovery. Apparently there is a really well preserved palace beneath, and the off-duty guys spend their time stealing artifacts. DAESH has plenty of cash, but I don't think the line troops are getting any of it. These guys seem to be helping themselves. Ferhad, Kevi's son, says the off-duty troops sleep down in the tunnels when they aren't scavenging. We're only going to have to deal with ten or twelve at the most as long as we hit this place hard and fast."

Brad rubbed his eyes. It had been a long and grueling day for all of them emotionally as well as physically.

"I need to sleep on this, guys. It's beginning to sound like a hundred other ops we've been on, a simple P.O.W. snatch ... a lightning strike, grab Murph, and run like hell." He shook his head slowly. "It sounds too easy, and both of you know that 'easy' ops are bullshit fairy tales. There have to be three different stages to this: the approach, the strike, and the flight ... and you can bet your ass disaster is gonna kick us in the stomach on at least one phase. It's like a law of nature."

"Murphy's Law," Ving quipped. The pun was greeted with a couple of wry smiles from Brad and Jared.

"Rack out, guys, I'll take the first watch," Brad said.

"Here, take this," Ving said, handing Brad the M-249. "There ain't but one narrow way into this hole and that's the trapdoor. With this thing you could hold off a small army."

Brad stood up and checked the safety on the SAW and then strode over to the bottom of the staircase leading to the trapdoor. Vicky followed him, carrying one of the lanterns. Ving and Jared stretched out on the hard carpeted floors and were almost immediately asleep, like the good grunts they were. They believed the old adage that sleep was a weapon, and over the years they had developed the knack of sleeping anywhere, any time, at the drop of a hat.

* * *

"Do you think this Kevi guy's information is reliable, Brad?"

"Jared is a good judge of character, Vicky, one of the best, and I trust him. If Jared says the intel is good, that's enough for me."

Vicky shook her head, a little awed at the unshakeable faith Brad had in his little band of comrades. She had encountered such a closely knit band of brothers only a couple of times in her experiences with special operations types, but she never encountered it to such a degree as she had seen in the Dallas team. Brad continued placing a lot of faith in Jared's judgment and it didn't seem to faze him in the least. She was surprised to find that she trusted Jared's judgment, too, considering the fact that her life depended on that same judgment.

"I trust his judgment, but we're going to do a recon of our own to confirm what Nahai told him," Brad continued. "Too much of a chance that things have changed. At least we have an idea what to look for."

Vicky settled down next to Brad and leaned her head on his shoulder. She approved of his caution. She told herself that she was just closing her eyes for a moment, but she fell fast asleep seconds later.

*   *   *

She was startled awake by Brad's sudden movement. She opened her eyes to see him kneeling on the stairs beside her, holding the SAW at the ready, thumbing off the safety, and staring at the trap door. A split second later she heard the sound of footsteps overhead and loud voices yelling in Arabic. She eased the Czech pistol into her hand without consciously thinking about it. She was tense and a little afraid despite her absolute faith in Brad's abilities.

She wondered if she should wake the others and glanced back nervously at them. She needn't have worried; they were all awake and silently scrambling for the weapons on the conference table. The yelling and the movement above seemed to last forever, although in actuality it could not have been more than a couple of minutes. The DAESH troops were conducting a frenzied building to building search, and they were careless. The trap door was not discovered.

It took a while for Team Dallas to settle down and get back to sleep. It was only a couple of hours later on Jared's watch when they were awakened once more, this time by the sound of American voices overhead. The voices were more subdued, and the search took longer, but again the trapdoor remained undiscovered.

*   *   *

Jared argued that it would be best if he went alone on the reconnaissance, that he would stand less chance of detection that way. Ving argued just as vehemently that he should go along with the SAW so that he could supply fire support in the event that Jared was detected. In the end, Brad decided that it would be best to go with stealth over firepower, but he also decided to go along on the recon. They could communicate by text message over the DTEK60s, but there was no way for them to cover the distance between their hideout and the ruins of the mosque fast enough if Jared should get in a jam.

They left the cellar as soon as it reached full dark outside. The trip down the now familiar alleyway had gone without incident. They'd been forced to move westward in the shadows of an unoccupied building along the edge of another greensward to the rear of some other buildings that fronted Al Markaz Road to reach the final obstacle to their objective.

The final obstacle was another four-lane boulevard, which presented them with yet another risk of exposure when they had to cross it. The last building before the roadway had been gutted by some kind of explosion. Since they had no binoculars, they negotiated the ruined stairs inside to what remained of the roof in order to get a better look at the crumbling remains of the Mosque of the Prophet Jonah atop the small hill across the street.

"It's still too far away for me to be certain, Brad," Jared whispered as they lay prone side by side atop the building. Several sentries were clearly visible against the light-colored stone and blocks of the ruins. They were strolling idly along the concrete drive that rose to the top of the mound and among the rubble strewn about by the massive explosion that had nearly leveled the ancient mosque. They looked obviously bored and did not appear to expect to have to defend themselves.

"Jesus, they sure made a mess of that place," Brad muttered. "They must have either had a real pro of a demolition man or else used a ton of explosives..."

"Both it looks like to me, Brad."

Brad sighed softly.

"I don't really want to do this, but we have to. We need to know if Murph is still there. I'm perfectly willing to risk going up there after him, but I'm not going to commit the others until I know for a fact that he's still there."

Jared scrutinized the roadway beneath them, observing several burned out hulks of vehicles scattered around the street.

"Looks like somebody managed to acquire some kind of rocket launcher. RPG maybe or maybe some LAWs."

"The Iraqi general that ordered his troops to abandon all that crap ought to be publicly horsewhipped," Brad muttered angrily.

"Or worse," Jared agreed. "I think we can use those burned out wrecks to cross that street."

"I don't think we have any other choice, buddy. Let's do it before I chicken out."

*   *   *

Brad lay face down in the deep shadow of a particularly large chunk of stone wall near the top of the hill, holding his breath. One of the sentries casually walked to within a few feet of where he was lying and stopped. The man had a cheap Chinese copy of an AK-47 slung across his shoulder, which led Brad to believe that he held a low status in Kavoosi's little group.

There had been little sign of a shortage of high quality weapons among the DAESH troops, but evidently they gave new or inexperienced recruits—or duds—the few inferior weapons they possessed. The sentry proved Brad's assumption a moment later by fumbling in his pockets and coming out with a crumpled pack of American cigarettes and a silver Zippo type lighter. Smoking was proscribed by DAESH for religious reasons, and possession of tobacco products remained a serious violation of their rules. The guy had to be a fuckup. New recruits were usually religious fanatics.

It took the sentry at least ten minutes to finish his smoke, but to Brad it felt like an eternity. The coal of the cigarette glowed intensely every time the man took a puff. In the end, a voice called out and the sentry quickly snuffed out the cigarette, tearing the paper and tobacco off the filter and scattering them. Then he wadded up the filter and tossed it into the rubble as he answered the voice.

"Over here!" He spoke in a normal tone of voice and Brad could hear him clearly.

"Smoking again, Rahim? Hamid will skin you if he catches you!" They were speaking in Farsi.

"He will not catch me. He is far too busy tormenting our infidel guest right now."

"Keep your voice down, Rahim! Do you not care if he hears you? The cell is only a camel's fart away from where you stand, and he just sent me out to see if all is secure. He's going to bring the prisoner outside for a few minutes of fresh air."

The sentry grunted and moved towards the sound of the voice.

"He surely wants to keep the prisoner healthy enough to collect that ransom money."

"Fool! Hamid does not care about the money. Mark my words, he has other plans for the infidel. Plans that require him to be standing and recognizable by the news cameras."

"Another beheading video?" the sentry asked in an amused tone.

"That is not for us to know, Rahim. Best you should leave the speculation to others and just do your job!"

Brad's ears perked up, and he crawled forward, silently as a snake, to peek around the chunk of rubble at the two sentries. He had managed to crawl within a few feet of the top of the hill undetected, and what little remained intact of the mosque looked only about thirty feet away.

As if on cue, the last cell door opened and Brandon Murphy was shoved through the doorway, landing in a heap in a bare dirt spot amid the rubble. The sound of laughter wafted through the night air and Hamid Kavoosi stepped out of the cell. Kavoosi was grinning and stroking his heavy beard.

"Enjoy the night air, infidel. You will not see another moon. When daylight comes, you will become another object lesson to those who oppose us. Your news reporters are our greatest asset, the parasites love to cover our beheadings."

Brad was sorely tempted to go ahead and take the shot, there were only three hostiles in sight, including Kavoosi. The temptation quickly subsided when two more hostiles emerged from out of nowhere and approached the two sentries.

Brad sighed inwardly. Taking the shot would have been foolish anyway. Jared was somewhere out in the darkness on the other side of the ruins, and a shot would have alerted the other sentries, making it much harder to get away. The new guys were obviously coming out to replace the sentries— shift change. The replacement sentries would be refreshed and more alert. The POW snatch would have a better chance of success in a few hours, when the boredom of the night lulled the replacements into a false sense of security. Brad glanced down at his chronometer. It was time to link up with Jared at the foot of the hill.

*   *   *

Brad sat at the conference table, huddled over the sack paper sketch with the stub of a pencil he had found in the desk, marking tentative positions on it. The plan he was formulating was a variation of one that Che Guevara used in the Cuban Revolution to defeat larger opponents with the small groups of guerillas under his command. The concept had been called the Minuet because it resembled a dance. The idea was to confuse the opponent by feigning an attack from one direction and then surprise them moments later by doing the same thing from a different direction. The plan permitted a very small group to completely befuddle a much larger unit by repeating the process at short intervals over and over.

He was hampered by the fact that he was limited to three teams instead of four, but he could not really count himself and Ving because they were going to conduct the actual snatch. It was critical to the plan that the direction they came from not be the same as one of the feints. Kavoosi's men needed to be facing anywhere except where Brad intended to approach from.

The faces of every member of the team showed utter confidence in him as he outlined the plan of attack for them. Only Ving and Jared noticed that he glossed over the getaway portion of the plan, but neither of them said anything. If Vicky recognized the shortcoming she didn't remark on it. Pete was experienced enough to have spotted the flaw, but he was still in pain from his wound. Brad knew him well enough to know that, when the shit hit the fan, Pete would grit it out and do whatever was necessary to get the job done.

When he had explained the plan and detailed each person's responsibilities thoroughly, he recommended that they relax for another hour and check their weapons again. It would be another hour or so before it would be time to begin to make their way back to the ruined mosque.

Brad wracked his brain for a solution to the escape portion of the plan. All hell was going to break loose when they hit Kavoosi's group, he was sure of that. The allied units in the area were already stirred up, and Brad felt equally sure that Kavoosi had alerted the other DAESH units nearby. His team had the claymores to use as a diversion, but there would not be time enough to place them far enough away to be an effective distraction. They had no way to detonate the claymores remotely; someone would have to press the clackers manually.

He was unhappy, and he was very much afraid that, despite the extraordinary skills of his team members, he might very well manage to snatch Murph from Kavoosi's clutches only to get them all killed while trying to get away, but he had to try. It was Murph's only chance since the bastards planned to behead him at daylight.

He pulled his BlackBerry out of a pocket and checked the charge on the battery. It was nearly out of power. Hmm.

NINETEEN

The claymores had been set up at the base of the hill where Brad and Jared had linked up earlier and the team had split up, Vicky with Pete, Charlie with Jessica, Ving with Brad, and Jared the lone wolf. They had moved slowly and carefully up the hill, using the rubble to conceal their passage. If Pete's wound was troubling him, he was doing a great job of concealing it.

Brad lay silently in the shadow of the same chunk of shattered masonry he had used earlier, waiting for the minute hand on his watch to sweep to the twelve position. It would be four a.m. in just a few more minutes, and the sentries appeared dull and listless. Human nature made most people susceptible to Circadian rhythms, and those rhythms dictated that the predawn hours would be the time when most people would be lethargic and slow to react. The adrenaline from the excitement of the climb up Mount Nebi Yunus served to circumvent the effects of Circadian rhythm in the team members, but the sentries had been standing guard for hours and they were bored out of their skulls.

As the sweep second hand and the minute hand of his chronograph struck twelve, two M-16s firing on full auto shattered the stillness of the night. Vicky and Pete were right on time. The sentries nearest Brad and Ving looked confused for a moment, and then, as rookies seemed prone to do, became drawn toward the sound of the gunfire.

The firing stopped as suddenly as it had started, and a startled silence settled over the hilltop for a moment before excited chattering from Kavoosi's men started. Forty-five seconds later, by Brad's chronograph, Charlie and Jessica's weapons opened up from a direction roughly one hundred twenty degrees away from Vicky and Pete's position. The confused sentries, seeking cover from the gunfire, moved slowly towards the new threat. Brad knew that Charlie and Jess would fire up two magazines in six to nine round bursts. Then they would fade back into the rubble, moving quickly towards the rendezvous point at the bottom of the hill where Vicky and Pete were supposed to be heading already. To add to the confusion, Jared would then initiate suppressive sniper fire from his vantage point in a nearby tree. As the firing started, Brad and Ving leaped to their feet and raced toward the cell where Murph was being held.

There was a guard posted outside the cell, but he was facing in the direction from which Charlie and Jessica were shooting. Without breaking stride Ving loosed a three-round burst from the SAW into his back and the sentry dropped to the ground in a bloody heap. Brad grabbed the iron bar on the cell door and slid it back then entered the room as Ving loosed another volley in the direction of one of the tunnel openings that led beneath the ruins.

"They're coming!" Ving yelled as Brad exploded into the cell.

*   *   *

Murph was startled awake by the rattle of small arms firing full auto outside his cell. He managed to get to one knee, his battered body aching even as adrenaline pumped through his system like a flash flood.

The door to the cell flew open and he was shocked to see a familiar face from his past.

"Well look what the cat dragged in," he said as he struggled to his feet. "What kept you?"

*   *   *

Brad and Ving had tossed several grenades as far as they could to add to the confusion as they hurried Murph down the hill towards the rendezvous point. Ving stumbled a few times on the way down as he was keeping an eye out behind them for Kavoosi's men. The diversion wouldn't hold them for long, and the pursuit would begin in earnest. The darkness would conceal the team's escape for only a short time. They would be hard pressed to get out of range before they could be seen clearly in the coming dawn ... but that was what the claymores were for.

The four other team members remained waiting at the rendezvous point as Brad herded Murph towards them.

"Go! Go! Go!" Brad shouted. All of them except Jared stood up and raced for the broad street, taking a path that would utilize the burnt out vehicle hulks in the street for cover or concealment. Brad and Murph had reached the far side of the street before the first claymore exploded with a deafening roar and an immense flash of light. They had managed another hundred yards before the second detonation occurred, and Brad heard the excited and confused screams in

Farsi after the sound died out. Jared was making the claymores count.

The team, one member short, reached the designated rally point in the lee of the shadows of the building Brad and Jared had climbed earlier during their reconnaissance just as the third of the claymores went off. They were all breathing hard from the run. Pete was silent, but he was pressing the bandana over his bullet wound. Murph was bent over, hands on his knees, as he struggled to catch his breath. He looked beat up, but otherwise he seemed fine.

"What are we waiting for?" he gasped.

"Jared," Brad replied, straining to see out in the darkness and blinking his eyes rapidly in an attempt to regain his night vision. The blood-red image of the exploding claymore was still imprinted on his retinas, and everything he saw was coming through a haze.

Less than thirty seconds later, they heard the sound of Jared's boots pounding on the greensward, and then the lanky Texan blew past them at full tilt.

"They're right behind me," he hollered unnecessarily. Brad and the rest of the team raced after him, herding Murph in front of them. Before they managed to reach the now familiar sight of the dumpster they had used to hide in, gunfire erupted less than a block away. Brad glance over at the doorway bearing the symbol Jared had showed him on the back of the kukri scabbard and made as if to lead the team over to it.

"No!" Jared barked. "He still lives there, and I don't intend to pay him back for his help by getting him killed!"

Brad altered his path without argument and raced toward their cellar hideout. The sound of gunfire increased. The sound of explosions shattered the early morning air followed by screams of "Allahu

Akbar!" A full scale battle had broken out and they were smack in the middle of it. Acrid smoke drifted down the alleyway and Brad knew it was only a matter of moments before the battle spilled in on top of them. The only option available was the hideout. He broke into a dead run for the back door of the building. The others knew instinctively where he was headed, and they rushed after him, Murphy in tow.

*   *   *

"You realize, of course, that there is no way we can stay here for long," Vicky said.

"I know, but I'm hoping the battle outside shifts. Any direction except north will work for us."

"DAESH is concentrated to the east of us," Ving said. "Their reinforcements will have to come from there. The allies are moving in from the west, so the battle will probably shift in either direction based on who's winning at the moment. Kavoosi's yo-yos are to the south, so the north is likely gonna be our best bet anyway."

"I hope so," Brad said fervently. "That's where the boat is and I don't really have a backup plan for getting the hell out of here." He turned to Murphy. "It's going to be tougher to get you out of here than I thought, buddy."

Murphy continued staring back and forth between the svelte redhead and the sexy young blonde in absolute confusion.

"What the hell?" he asked no one in particular.

"This is my team, Murph," Brad responded. "We didn't have anything else to do at the time, so when we saw you had become a television star we decided to pay you a visit."

Murph grinned.

"I see you're still crazy, Brad," he said. "Man, I've never been so glad to see anybody in my life!"

"Not a bit happier than we were to see you in that alley in Fallujah," Ving said, his voice cracking with emotion as he walked over to Murph and gave him a bear hug.

"Jeez Ving," Murph gasped as he returned the big man's hug. "If you don't take it easy I'll be just as dead as Kavoosi wanted me to be. Then you guys will have wasted a trip."

"You know him? His name I mean?" Brad asked.

"I didn't before he captured me or at least I only knew of his name before. I know a lot more about the bastard now. That crew spoke in Farsi the whole time they had me, and they never had a clue that I understood every word they were saying."

"Did you learn anything that might help us get out of this mess?" Jared asked.

"Yeah Jared, I learned enough about DAESH troop dispositions to know that Ving is probably right

about which way the battle outside is going to go. I
don't know much regarding the current strength of
the allied forces, but I know DAESH has a hell of a
lot of troops here. Mosul is their headquarters
now, and they've sent out a call to all the faithful to
come and make a stand here."

"Can you tell me why somebody in our
government tried to keep me from getting you out
of here?" Brad asked.

Murphy snorted. "That bastard!" He shook his
head sadly. "How could he even have known I was
going to get captured? I had no idea I was going to
get separated from that Iraqi special ops team until
it actually happened!" He paused for a moment,
and it appeared obvious that he was thinking hard.
"I knew he had a monster deal cooking, but I didn't
think even he would be willing to let me die over
it."

"Who?"

"Willingham."

"Duncan Willingham?" Vicky asked.

"Duncan is just the government connection. But there is no doubt in my mind it's his brother Parker who's jerking his strings."

"Who the hell is Duncan Willingham?" Brad asked, bewildered.

"He's the C.I.A. station chief assigned to Mosul," Vicky interrupted. "He's a sleazy dirtbag with some highly questionable friends in the State Department. The Justice Department has been trying to pin something on him for years, but he's slippery as hell."

"And Parker Willingham is the new owner of Belus Security," Brad finished for her. "I heard rumors he was as bad as his predecessor, but I had no idea..."

"I told you," Ving snorted, "but no, you wouldn't listen to me..."

"Don't get your panties in a wad, Ving. I was not going to repeat rumors, even one you strongly suspect is true. Not without proof."

"He's dirty all right," Murphy said. "I would have reported him—should have reported him—but I knew his brother was the station chief. I figured I might have more success reporting him back in the States after my contract runs out next month." His face had turned red with shame. The truth was that if he had ratted out the owner he would have lost his completion bonus, a substantial amount of tax-free cash that would have permitted him to retire from the dirty business he was in. The years had taken a toll on his body, and he had been desperate to get out of the rat race.

"Reported him for what, Murph?"

"I inadvertently overheard a conversation between Parker and the deputy commander of DAESH in Mosul. I didn't know who he actually was until later, when I recognized his photo in a briefing, but I did know he was DAESH."

"And the meeting was about…" Brad kept pressing.

"He wanted Parker to have us, Belus, hinder the efforts of the Iraqis and the friendlies," Murphy said, shamefaced. "It was a shitload of money, Brad."

"He wanted Belus contractors to fire on American troops?" Brad asked, outraged.

"He didn't come right out and say, 'Fire on them,' Brad, but I got the impression that was what he wanted. I… I let it go because I was attached to a Golden Division Special Forces team, and I knew damned well I would never fire on U.S. troops. I knew he couldn't make me do that."

The disappointment in the eyes of Brad, Ving, and Jared was almost more than he could bear.

"Parker Willingham is supposed to meet with the guy in just a few days to finalize the deal," Murph said, desperate to regain his former comrades' goodwill. "I have the exact date and time written down in my journal back at my billet."

Brad's face remained impassive. After a long pause, he spoke, slowly and clearly. His was no longer the tone of an old and trusted comrade-in-arms, it was the tone of a very disappointed former friend.

"If we manage to get you out of here in one piece, that journal might help you avoid prosecution, Murphy. I have to extract my team from this predicament that I put them in because of my debt to you, but when we get out—if we get out—you can consider my debt to you repaid. Have I made myself clear?"

"Crystal," Murphy said, his cheeks still burning with shame.

*   *   *

"There was no way you could have known, Brad."
Vicky was sitting beside him in a far corner of the
room away from the others.

"It doesn't matter. They're all here, at risk, because
I owed Murph my life."

"Not just you, Brad," Ving said. He had walked up
to the two of them unnoticed. He could move with
amazing stealth for such a large man. "I owed him
too." It was very out of character for Ving to speak
with such bitterness in his voice.

Brad shook his head sadly. "Jess, Vicky, Charlie,
Pete..."

"Don't include me in your guilt trip, Brad. I'll
consider this whole thing worthwhile if I can put a
nail in Duncan Willingham's coffin." Vicky's face
was stony.

"If I can figure a way out of this crap," Brad said. A look of stubborn determination spread over his face and he stood up, making his way toward the staircase.

"Where are you going?" Vicky asked, alarm on her face.

"I need to check and see if the battle outside has shifted yet. The sooner we can move toward the boat the better our chances of getting out of here alive."

Ving and Vicky wanted to argue with him, but they both knew him well enough to know that argument would be useless. They watched him as he climbed the stairs, lifted the trap door, and disappeared.

*   *   *

The acrid smell of gun smoke permeated the building, and the flickering light from flames out in the street cast the shadows of frenzied dancing flames on the dirty paint of the stucco walls in the long room. The rattle of gunfire and the sounds of explosions were further away than they had been earlier, toward the east, which tended to make Brad think that, for the moment, DAESH had the upper hand. He also knew that, with upwards of seventy thousand troops in and around Mosul, the tide would turn against DAESH at any moment. It was time to go, and it was time to go in a hurry.

*   *   *

They were outside, and they were moving as fast as Pete's leg could manage. There was little more than twelve hundred feet in a straight line from their hideout to the spot where they had beached the dory under the bridge. But the presence of walking wounded and stragglers caused Brad to lead the team westwards for two blocks before turning back towards the north and the Khosr River. Time and again they were engaged by ambulatory DAESH troops, but between Jared's accurate fire and the withering fire from the SAW, they managed to move ahead.

No one had offered to give Murphy a weapon. As a matter of fact, since his revelation in the cellar no one seemed willing to even talk to him. He stopped along the way and lifted the web gear from a fallen DAESH trooper and took the dead man's M-16 as well. He was undoubtedly a sonofabitch, but he was a skilled warrior, and he gave a good account of himself, protecting the team's flank and acting as rear guard.

Brad led them to the southern edge of the roadway that bordered the Khosr River and held up his fist in the sign that told them to stop and secure their perimeter, which they did instantly. Puzzled, Jared crawled forward to rest beside Brad, who was lying flat, scrutinizing the roadway to the left and right. It was easily apparent to both of them that the fighting had been particularly heavy along this stretch.

The mouth of the bridge was littered with still burning vehicles, and there were literally hundreds of bodies scattered along the pavement. Not all the bodies were dead. Here and there an arm fluttered or a leg bent. In several places wounded men were assisting others in much worse shape. The fighting had been fierce.

"How the hell are we going to get down to the damned boat?" Jared whispered.

"Fast," Brad muttered. "Pass the word. Lock and load fresh magazines, ready however many grenades we have left, and get ready to run like hell."

"Brad, there's no way Pete's going to be able to run on that leg…"

"I'll stick with Pete, Jared. You lead the others down to the boat and then do what you can to cover us until I can get Pete down there."

"Brad, I can't leave you..."

"You *will* do exactly as I told you, Jared," Brad said firmly. His arm went out to Jared's shoulder and their eyes locked. "I am *counting* on you to make sure that Jess and Vicky get to that boat, you hear me?"

"Yeah, I got it," Jared said. His pained expression reflected his dislike of the command he had just received as well as his recognition that it was in fact a *command.* "Semper Fi, Brad," he said, his voice unsteady.

"Semper Fi, buddy," Brad replied. He remained on the ground as Jared stood and motioned the others forward. When Pete hobbled to the front, Brad stood and lifted Pete's arm over his shoulder. "Let's go, Pete. This is gonna hurt like hell, but it has to be done." Without another word, they began to run after the others. The distance between them and the rest of the team grew larger with every step they took.

The team had almost reached the bridge when Murphy realized that Brad and Pete weren't with them. He turned and began to run back towards the two men. Brad tried to wave him off, but Murphy kept coming. He was almost back to them when one of the wounded DAESH troops by the side of the road leaned up on one arm and raised the muzzle of his M-16 towards Murphy.

Murphy shot him though the chest without slowing down. When he reached Brad and Pete, he slipped under Pete's free arm and began to run with them, the pistol grip of his confiscated rifle in his right hand and his appropriated and ill fitted web gear flopping against his body as they ran. Brad didn't even try to chew him out, he needed his breath to keep running. He was pissed though.

*   *   *

Murphy's shot had alarmed them, but they hadn't turned back. Jared was driving them forward. Everyone in the team had thrown themselves to the ground when they'd reached the dory, facing back towards Brad, Pete, and Murphy anxiously.

"I didn't realize they were so far behind," Vicky gasped in horror.

Jared unlimbered the big Weatherby, which he'd carried slung over his shoulder since they had begun the approach to the mosque, and wrapped the sling around his arm. The Leupold scope captured an incredible amount of light, and it was beginning to be bright enough to use it. It was a magnificent weapon, and Kevi had given it to him, which made it doubly precious to him. It was also helpful in spotting wounded soldiers trying to take a shot at the three running men.

The scope helped him spot the movement, but when he acquired a target, Jared's master eye dropped to the iron sights. There wasn't time for all the steps required for serious sniping. His finger made a swift but controlled pull on the trigger and the big rifle roared.

A figure behind Brad and the other two men exploded in a shower of blood and gore. Jared's lanky frame absorbed the massive recoil, and he quickly brought the barrel down to bear on another target. His operation of the finely jeweled bolt was swift and masterful, and a third round was downrange before any of the team realized he was going to shoot again.

Brad, Pete, and Murphy reached the team as Jared was reloading the three-round magazine. If there were any other shooters able to fire at the team they had been dissuaded by the geysers of blood and bone following the three shots.

"I don't think we're going anywhere in this boat, guys."

They turned as one to look at Charlie, who was lying on the ground beside the bow of the boat. The hull of the boat had been riddled with large caliber rounds. To Brad it looked as if someone had fired it up with one of the truck mounted .50 caliber machine guns that they had seen on the black trucks, which was precisely what had happened.

"Shit!" he grumbled, a sinking feeling in the pit of his stomach. There was no way the boat would ever float again. It didn't even look as if it could be repaired.

As if the destruction of their only way out of Nineveh was not enough bad luck, the angry drone of several of the black trucks could be heard speeding towards the bridge. They couldn't fight from the bank of the river, they were surrounded by high ground and they were trapped like fish in a barrel. The sinking feeling in Brad's stomach got worse.

"We're screwed," Murphy said quietly.

Brad's spirit refused to give up. Improvise, adapt, overcome. The words were branded on his soul. In all probability he had led his team into a trap from which they could not escape, but he was not about to go down without a fight.

"Ving!" he barked.

"Yeah?" Ving was calmly loading the end of one of the bandoliers into the M-249.

"Did any of those hulks on the bridge look like maybe one of the pedestal mounted guns might still be in working order?"

"Damn Brad! I didn't even think of that... Yeah, probably."

"Let's get up top, buddy," Brad said, standing up. "I don't feel like dying down here." He glanced first at Jessica and then at Vicky. "Find someplace to hide and stay..."

"Don't even think about it, Brad Jacobs!" Jessica stormed. "I know what these people do to women they capture. I'd rather die on the bridge with you than submit to that!"

Vicky glared at him, but all she could manage to say was, "Ditto!"

As one, they moved to the top of the bridge. Far down the boulevard they could see the black trucks, a half dozen of them, racing towards their position. There was no place to run that they could reach before the trucks would be on top of them.

Ving climbed atop one of the trucks that had wrecked but had not burned and was jerking the charging handle back on the mounted .50 caliber machine gun.

"Not a lot of ammo left, Brad, but this baby is a go!" Ving said with a grin. He handed the SAW down to Pete, who was leaning against the rear wheel well. He then passed the web gear with its loaded ammunition pouches to him. Pete hobbled over to one of the trucks that had burned and painfully climbed up into the bed and took up a firing position. The others took up positions behind the other wrecks and faced the oncoming trucks, which were still out of range of their M-16s.

The massive roar from Jared's Weatherby startled all of them except Ving, who followed Jared's example and sent three rounds from the big .50 downrange. Jared's shot struck the lead truck first, impacting the radiator and sending a cloud of steam shooting into the air. The .50 caliber rounds struck next, the first one striking the pavement roughly twenty feet in front of the truck. The next struck beneath the front bumper, and the third blew out the windshield in front of the driver who immediately disappeared in a gout of red mist.

Jared was already firing at the following truck, and Ving was aiming at the one beside it. The trucks kept coming, and Ving and Jared kept shooting. Soon there were only two trucks still coming, but they looked almost within range of the smaller rifles. Elated by the success of the two big guns, the others brought their weapons up, ready to engage the last two trucks.

It was Jared who first noticed the ground troops emerging from the trees lining the road intersecting the main boulevard at an angle nearly eight hundred feet south of their bridgehead. There were only about thirty of them. But they had heard the roar of the Weatherby and the .50 and they were taking cover, advancing on the bridgehead, leapfrogging from covered position to covered position the way infantrymen the world over are trained to do.

"Shit!" Jared exclaimed. "Look at your two o'clock!"

Brad's heart, on the rise because of their initial successes, sank into his feet. His team was outnumbered, and they had already expended most of the ammunition they had. Grimly, he raised his rifle to firing position and took careful aim at one of the lead soldiers. He squeezed off a round and watched the man fall.

"Single shots!" He yelled to the others. "Aim! Make every shot count!" He fired once more, and another soldier hit the grass. The others followed his instructions to the letter. The oncoming troops slowed down as their fellows began to drop, and the leapfrogging slowed down even more, exactly as Brad had known it would. Not that it mattered. Team Dallas was outnumbered, out-gunned, and out of luck. Barring a miracle, which was something Brad did not believe in, they were all dead within the next few minutes.

TWENTY

Hank Guzman had been on the ready line, doing a walk around preflight of the remanufactured UH-1 "Huey" he had been assigned by the Iraqi Army. There were four of them in his flight, all of them repurposed from their initial mission of Search and Rescue to gunship. Hank cut his teeth flying "Hueys", and that was the main reason why his current employer, a private military contractor out of Destin, Florida had hired him.

The Iraqis purchased the choppers from the U.S. government to conduct Medevac and Search and Rescue missions. The Hueys had been sent to a factory just outside Panama City, Florida to be reconditioned before being flown to the Port City of Mobile, Alabama for shipment to the Port of Basra in Iraq when the country was still being run by Saddam Hussein. Hussein had been a merciless bastard, but he treated the helicopters better than he had treated his people. He hired American technicians to maintain the birds and paid them lavishly to keep them in Iraq. No money had been spared in the maintenance of the venerable helicopters.

Consequently, the Hueys were in magnificent condition. The current Iraqi government had ordered them repurposed into gunships and turned over to the private military contractor Hank worked for at Erbil International Airport. The Iraqis were prohibited by law from operating in Iraqi Kurdistan, and they desperately needed air support there. The PMC was the logical solution.

This morning, Hank's flight was scheduled to support ground troops in Mosul for a scheduled push into the area of the ancient City of Nineveh, which was now a part of the City of Mosul. About a half hour before sunrise, during his preflight inspection, the cell phone Brad Jacobs had given him alerted him to an incoming series of text messages. Text messages are limited to one hundred and forty characters, so multiple messages are not uncommon. Not wanting to appear unprofessional, Hank hurried, but hurried carefully, through the rest of the preflight before stepping off the flight line and checking the messages.

The first message contained GPS coordinates and the word "Extraction." The second message was a question: "Possible these cords @ sunrise?" A third message read: "POW snatch, sitrep: sticky."

Hank, from long experience with Brad, interpreted the messages as "We are conducting a POW snatch predawn and need to be extracted at sunrise from this location because the situation could be difficult. Is this possible?"

Concerned, Hank pulled an acetate-covered 1:25,000 topographical map from the thigh pocket on his flight suit, mentally converting the GPS coordinates to map coordinates as he did so, even though he already had a general idea of the location. It was within ten kilometers of the place he was scheduled to rendezvous with a forward observer for the Iraqi 38th or "Golden" Division. The Golden Division was the Spearhead of Iraqi Special Operations Forces, not to be confused with Special Forces, which are elite airborne troops highly trained for clandestine or covert unconventional missions. The Golden Division consisted of troops specializing in urban warfare, house to house fighting against DAESH troops and liberating cities.

Hank felt a surge of excitement. It sounded as if Brad was about to snatch Brandon Murphy from his captors. Brad had never been the kind of guy who was overly optimistic, and Hank felt that the man had been pretty sure of succeeding or he wouldn't have placed the request. The time requested was about fifteen minutes prior to Hank's scheduled rendezvous and only ten klicks out of his way. He would have found a way to go to

Brad anyway, but this way he could kill two birds with one stone.

And he could let Pete take the copilot's seat for a few ground support runs, just for old times' sake. The two had flown together in the old days before Hank had retired from active duty. He grinned. How lucky could a guy get? Quickly he selected Brad's number from the contact menu and texted the message, "Wilco," meaning, "message received and understood, will comply." He had no idea that Brad never received his response because the battery in his BlackBerry had died.

*   *   *

Even though DAESH maintained no airpower to speak of, Hank and the other chopper pilots had to keep a close watch for ground troops with RPGs and LAWs rockets. That task is not quite as difficult as it sounds. Visual acuity from cruising height in a Huey is amazing, and the sharp-eyed have little difficulty in distinguishing between ordinary rifles and shoulder launched rockets or rocket grenade launchers. Compared to other places Hank Guzman had flown combat missions, Iraq was a breeze.

Flight time from Erbil to Mosul in a Huey was less than half an hour, and Hank had little trouble amending his flight plan to allow for an earlier departure. The flight of four lifted off while it was still dark on the ground, but at a cruising altitude of sixteen hundred feet, visibility looked virtually the same as it was in daylight. Darkness actually rises from the ground because darkness is simply the shadow cast by the earth itself. High above the ground, there is usually always light from the sun.

The sound of the turbine engine sounded awesome, and the controls felt sweet in his hand. The Huey was crabbing at a slight angle due to the crosswind, but that was normal. Hank was feeling just fine.

His first feelings of apprehension came when the skyline, or what was left of it, of Mosul came into view through his Perspex windscreen. The smoke of battle was rising from the north end of the city, smoke from a battle that should not have started already. He quickly switched frequency on his air-to-ground radio and heard the excited chatter coming over the airwaves. Something was wrong. He tried the call sign for his forward observer/ground control contact and received no response. He increased his forward speed and ordered his gunner to lock and load.

*   *   *

Brad wiped the cold sweat from his eyes. He was down to his last thirty-round magazine. Jared had run out of cartridges for the Weatherby and had slung it across his back and was firing the M-16 he acquired from Nahai. Ving's .50 had run dry, and he was firing his M-16 from behind the cab of the truck that the .50 was mounted on.

"Ammo check!" Brad screamed over the sound of the guns. One by one the team responded. Jessica was already out, and the rest were down to either one or two magazines. Still the DAESH troops were advancing, one and two meters at a time.

In sheer desperation he looked in every direction for anything he could use to put off the inevitable. His eyes lit on the body of the first man Jared had shot with the Weatherby. The corpse was lying flat on its back, belly to the sky. The web belt he wore was tattered and bloody—the web belt!

*   *   *

Jared was watching Brad when the team leader's eyes locked on something on the side of the road to the north of the bridge. Dawning comprehension flickered in his eyes and he stopped thinking. In a flash he stripped the Weatherby from around his neck and he was running like hell towards the body of the first of the Weatherby's victims. Not only was Jared the fastest member of Team Dallas, he was closest to the north side of the bridge and to the bodies of a bunch of dead DAESH troops.

As soon as he was out from behind the relative safety of the wrecked truck, he bent over into a crouch, trying to make himself as small a target as possible. He swerved to the left, paralleling the retaining wall between the roadway and the riverbed. He reached the dead soldier and ripped the web gear from the corpse, tossing it over the retaining wall. He low crawled to the next body and tapped the magazine pouches. They were full. He ripped his web gear off as well and tossed it over the wall and down to the green grass below.

At least one of the DAESH troops assaulting the bridgehead had noticed him and continued firing at him slowly and deliberately. Bullets were kicking up pavement all around him, but luckily the soldier was a lousy shot. Jared wondered how long his luck would hold. He also wondered if Brad would understand why he was tossing the web gear over the retaining wall. Putting his thoughts out of his head, Jared continued to collect more web gear.

*   *   *

Brad knew why Jared had run from his firing position to the bloody corpse on the side of the road. What he didn't understand at first was why in the hell Jared was tossing the web gear he retrieved over the retaining wall. It seemed insane. The real reason struck him at about the same time he saw Jared's body jerk when a projectile fired by a DAESH M-16 struck him. The retaining wall dropped nearly three feet below the roadbed, getting progressively deeper until it leveled out at the riverbed ... out of the line of sight of the DAESH troops.

*   *   *

Jared felt the burning sting of the bullet as it tore into the meaty part of his right buttock. He didn't even think, he simply got a firm hold of the web gear on the body in front of him and rolled over the edge of the retaining wall and onto the relatively safe grass there, the body falling on top of him. The man—the kid actually, he couldn't have been more than sixteen—was lying on top of him, his eyes slowly glazing over. He wasn't dead yet.

The kid managed to utter just two words in Arabic before he gasped and died. The words were, "Help me."

Pushing the pitiful scene from his mind, Jared turned over and removed the kid's web gear then crawled back along the retaining wall collecting the sets of gear he had dropped over the side. There were five in all. Ignoring the pain that was just then beginning to register in his butt cheek, he ran crouched over towards the bridge, protected from enemy fire by the retaining wall, safe in the depression of the river bed.

*   *   *

In complete amazement, Brad watched as Jared ran towards the north side of the bridge with an armload of web gear, hopefully containing precious ammunition in the ammo pouches. Ving saw Jared, too, and he leaped down from his firing position and leaned over the concrete bridge rail, lifting first the ammo pouches Jared held up then Jared himself by one arm, up and over the rail.

Ving tried to check Jared's wound first, but Jared waved him off, pointing at the ammo pouches. Understanding, Ving ripped the pouches open and tore out the STANAG magazines, checking each to see if it was charged, and tossing the empties out onto the bridge surface. Of the thirty magazines in the pouches, fourteen were empty and useless. Dropping two magazines beside Jared, Ving moved into a combat crouch and distributed the magazines to everyone else. He had the SAW, so he kept the two extra for himself.

*   *   *

Brad had not seen Jared drag himself back to his firing position and shove a magazine into the empty magazine well of his M-16. The DAESH troops kept coming in dribs and drabs, one or three at a time from around the trees lining the road the rest had come from. The team was keeping up remarkably, with few wasted shots, but the hostiles kept coming in a seemingly endless trickle.

Ving was pretty effective, conserving his ammo by restricting his automatic fire to two and three-round bursts, something only a true expert could manage without causing a malfunction. Despite Jared's sacrifice, and their effective fire, the team was soon running low on ammunition again. The hostiles continued to dribble in and continue the attack. One by one, first Jessica, then Charlie, then

Vicky, the whole team, watched the bolts on their rifles lock open.

In despair, Brad glanced over at Vicky. Her face looked sad and grim, but she reached for the holster on her web belt and pulled out the Czech pistol. She looked him straight in the eyes and pointed first at the pistol, then at Jessica, and then at her own head. Brad's heart hurt. He understood. Vicky would not submit to the indignity of rape and torture at the hands of the hostiles, nor would she allow Jessica to suffer it either. Brad nodded his head in agreement and looked away. He couldn't watch. There was no longer a single molecule of hope left in him. Behind him, he heard Ving curse aloud as he fired the last round in the SAW. It was over.

*   *   *

Hank was pushing his chopper at the limits of its speed. He was close enough to see the units on the ground beneath him fully engaged. Still unable to contact his forward observer, he searched for the bridge at the coordinates Brad had given him. There were people fighting from the bridgehead, battling against perhaps two dozen hostiles.

From his vantage point high in the air, he could see what the ground combatants could not. A much larger force, numbering a hundred or more, was approaching the bridge from behind a row of trees along the roadside. In a matter of minutes, the bridgehead would be overrun and, unless Brad had lied or made an egregious error, the defenders of the bridgehead were Brad and his team, Hank's friends.

There was no hesitation in him. Hank signaled for the other three choppers to follow him, followed by the signal for a gun run. The door gunners tightened their body straps and leaned into the swivel mounted M-60 machine guns in the open doors. Hank banked sharply to the right, swinging out past the bridge and then back to the left in a one hundred eighty degree turn, dropping to around three hundred feet and slowing down to about sixty miles per hour over the ground.

"Fire! Fire! Fire!" he yelled into his headset. In the doors, the gunners began the lethal business of killing.

*   *   *

Brad was first to hear the familiar sound of the Huey rotor blades chopping the air with their distinctive sound. He spotted them coming, in a modified "V" formation, and he knew his text to Hank had gotten through. The whirlybirds were headed straight for the bridgehead, low and fast.

"Wait!" he screamed at Vicky, pointing at the sky and continuing to scream at the top of his lungs.

Vicky, the Czech pistol still in her hand, turned to see the choppers coming straight at them. She waited until the choppers has swung past them and turned back to line up for a strafing run before she dropped the pistol and covered her face with her hands.

Charlie had taken Jessica into his arms and was holding her close to him, but Brad, Ving, Jared, Pete, and Murphy watched as the flight of Hueys began the first of three strafing runs. The magnificent guns in the doors blazed, sending down a lead rain of death on the hostiles. Shattered bodies piled up, more of them with each run. By the time the choppers circled for the third and last time, there was no one standing within sight of the bridgehead. While three of the birds circled overhead, the lead chopper dropped down to the roadway on top of the bridge behind the team's fighting positions, the rotors still turning.

Wasting no time, Brad herded them all to the bird, Charlie and Ving half carrying Jared and Murphy. The crew chief jumped out to the road surface and ushered Vicky and Jessica aboard before helping to shove Jared and Murphy inside. Brad and the others climbed in and the chopper lifted off before they could even buckle the belts provided for the safety of passengers.

TWENTY-ONE

Hank had helped them with the first embarrassing predicament they faced after the Mosul mission. He had been the one who pointed out that getting Jared medical attention for his increasingly painful gunshot wound could prove difficult and have possible legal repercussions. He had also provided a practical solution.

Using one of his employers' carryalls, he had driven the entire team to the civilian home of a former U.S. Army Special Forces medic. The retired sergeant first class had Military Occupational Specialty training that qualified him, as he cheerfully explained to them as he cleaned and patched the hole in Jared's butt cheek, to perform any surgical procedure up to, but not including, the opening of the human cranium. When he had finished with Jared and Pete, he addressed Murphy's various cuts, contusions and abrasions.

He checked for signs of internal bleeding, and, though he found none, he advised Murphy to see a regular physician at his earliest convenience. His last bit of cheerful advice was for Murphy to see a dentist about his broken teeth. The best part of the whole experience was that, even though Brad could see the curiosity on his face, the medic did not ask any questions. He also refused to take money for his services, even though Brad offered to pay him.

When Brad had offered the money, the medic finally asked two questions. "Jarheads, right?" Brad nodded. "Force Recon?" Brad nodded in the affirmative again.

"Semper Fi, buddy." The medic had taken his hand and shaken it. "Some of my best friends are Marines … but don't tell anybody." He started to turn away and then turned back to face Brad a final time. "Don't take this wrong, I've got nothing against Jarheads, but I wouldn't want my sister to marry one." With that remark, he turned away, laughing at his own joke.

"What was all that about?" Vicky asked, mildly indignant.

Brad grinned at her. "Nothing to worry about, baby. You should know by now that Green Beanies just ain't right."

*   *   *

The second problem they faced was a bit more complicated... What to do with Brandon Murphy? He was in the country legally, but he wasn't about to return to the control of his employer. As far as he was concerned, he was a marked man at Belus and Brad agreed with him. Neither of the Willingham brothers was a safe bet, and either or both of them wanted Murphy dead.

That meant that the C.I.A. wasn't safe to approach either. Ving suggested the ranking CENTCOM (U.S. Central Command, which maintained a forward headquarters at Al Udeid Air Base in Qatar) officer. But Murphy pointed out that the C.I.A. liaison officer to CENTCOM was also in titular charge of all the private military contractors in the Middle East and therefore suspect as well.

Surprisingly, it was Charlie who came up with the solution to the Murphy conundrum. He rode into work with Hank the day after they returned and contacted a close personal friend at the U.S. Department of State over a bona fide secure government line while the others remained at Hank's house.

Hank's wife Liz was a pleasingly plump grandmotherly type who knew enough not to ask any embarrassing questions. She really liked Vicky and Jessica and took a motherly shine to Jared. Either because of a natural dislike, or more likely because Hank had told her what he had done, she was definitely cold towards Brandon Murphy.

Brad had conflicting feelings about the man. He owed Murphy his life, though it could be argued that he had repaid that debt by saving Murphy's life. Even so, Brad was not the kind of man who could forget that kind of debt. As far as he was concerned, the saving of a life created a debt that could never be paid off. Saving Murphy's life had created a debt to Brad himself, but it did not absolve him in the least of his obligation to Murphy. To Brad, that was a lifetime obligation.

The conflict arose because of the other side of the same coin. Brad was also not the kind of man who could forgive betrayal. His personal moral code held that betrayal was the one true unforgivable sin. It was a conflict that he tried, with Vicky's help, to resolve ... unsuccessfully. Murphy had been willing to stand by and let American soldiers and Marines die for money. It was not an action Brad felt capable of ignoring.

The conflict was still unresolved when a man from the U.S. Consulate in Erbil with four U.S. marshals wearing sunglasses arrived at Hank's house to take Murphy into custody.

"From what I've been told," the official told Brad, "he's safer with us than he would be anywhere in the Middle East. The marshals are taking him into protective custody, and he will be transported back to the States on SecState's C-37 as soon as it arrives and is refueled tonight. He's really got a hard-on for the Willingham brothers, and this is the first time he's been able to get anybody, still alive anyway, willing to testify against either of them. I'd bet a dollar against a donut that your friend Murphy is going to get offered immunity for his testimony."

Brad's mouth twisted into a moue of distaste.

"He's not my friend … at least, not anymore."

The diplomat gave him a weird look but didn't say anything else.

*   *   *

Unwilling to trust even the U.S. Marshal's Service, at least in Iraq, Brad and Ving accompanied the limousine transporting Murphy to the consulate and then sat unspeaking beside him in a waiting room inside the consulate until it was time to transport him to the airport. Just before Murphy was to climb aboard the aircraft, he turned to Brad.

"I know you can't forgive me, and I understand why. I just want you to understand that I will not rest until they convict both of the Willinghams in a court of law. I swear it." He turned and walked aboard the C-37A, which was the military nomenclature for a stock Gulfstream V executive jet.

"You believe that crap, Brad?" Ving asked, his face an impassive mask.

"Yeah, I believe him ... but I still can't forgive him." He shook his head sadly. "He was a good friend for a long time, Ving. I thought I knew him."

Ving clapped Brad on the shoulder and rewarded him with a grin.

"I ain't studyin' that man no more. Come on, we need to get me home. Willona's going to be pissed because I didn't bring her anything back and I am in dire need."

"Dire need?" Brad asked, his eyebrows raised inquisitively. "Dire need of what?"

"Bacon, my man," Ving boomed in his deepest basso profundo voice. "I am suffering from a severe case of bacon deprivation. Do you realize, my friend, that the savage inhabitants of this hostile land refrain from indulging in the most refined and cultured culinary experience known to man?" He shook his great bald head in mock sadness. "They not only decline to consume the world's greatest gastronomic delight, they prohibit others from consuming it as well!" Ving could sound like a college professor when he wanted to. He was still bitching eloquently when they arrived back at Hanks's house.

EPILOGUE

Brad awakened in his own bed in his own home to a sensation he had only experienced once before in his life. His entire midsection was aflame with the most intense and incredible sensation he had ever felt ... warm, wet, and excruciatingly pleasurable.

"Jesus... Vicky... Baby..." he gasped.

She lifted her head. "You like?" she asked.

"You have to ask?" He was having trouble forming words to answer her. Twenty incredible minutes later, Vicky's head was lying on his chest, and he was lying, exhausted, on his pillow, too weak to even caress the soft skin of her back.

They had been back from Erbil less than twenty-four hours, and he was still jet lagged. Vicky didn't seem to be affected by it at all.

She sat up in the bed and reached over for a short satin shirt that reached to mid-thigh, exposing a vast expanse of creamy thigh when she stood up. There were buttons down the front, but she never fastened them unless she had to answer the doorbell. Even then she only buttoned it up to her sternum. Vicky was an incurable exhibitionist.

She stepped out of the bed and reached over for his jeans, which he'd left folded over the back of his bedroom chair.

"Time to get up, sleepyhead," she said, chuckling. "Ving called while you were asleep."

Brad sat up in the bed.

"He did? When?"

"About forty-five minutes ago," she replied, walking towards the bathroom, her hips swinging invitingly. Despite their recent amorous activity, Brad felt a stirring. "I'm going to take a shower," she said. "Are you going to join me?"

He didn't wait to answer her; ten seconds later, he was standing behind her in the shower, soaping her shoulders.

"What did he want?" he asked.

"Who?" she responded. She turned to face him and laughed delightedly at the expression on his face. "I'm just teasing you, baby. Ving said he and Willona were going to come right over."

"Forty-five minutes ago they were coming right over?"

Vicky took the soap from his hands and began to soap him down.

"Relax, baby, I told him to give us a couple of hours."

"What did he want?" Vicky was impossible to resist when she was like this. As much as he hated to be teased, Vicky managed to turn it into a pleasure.

"He said Willona wants to 'refine' some of the terms of the contract."

Brad groaned.

"He also said to tell you he wants bacon when he gets here. He said he's suffering from something called bacon deficit disorder and that it's your fault."

Brad groaned again.

"I don't know which I dread more, negotiating with Willona or listening to Ving's jokes."

Vicky hugged him.

"You don't dread Ving's jokes, baby. You say you do, but you don't. You need to treasure that man. There aren't enough like him in our world." She was deadly serious. "He's that rarest of creatures, a true friend. There aren't many like him."

"No, there aren't," Brad said softly. "Not many at all." He was thinking of Brandon Murphy. He still couldn't bring himself to forgive the man, but he honestly hoped that Murph managed to get through his testimony against the Willinghams before they had him killed. It was a sad but well known truth that people with as much money as Parker Willingham could get away with almost anything.

THE END.

Thank you for taking the time to read TRACK DOWN IRAQ. If you enjoyed it, please consider telling your friends or posting a __short review__. Word of mouth is an author's best friend and much appreciated. Thank you, Scott Conrad

EXCLUSIVE SNEAK PEEK: TRACK DOWN BORNEO – BOOK 5

William Darnell Duckworth IV, "Bill" to his very few friends and CEO of Duckworth International Petroleum to everyone else, landed at Brunei International Airport in Bandar Seri Begawan and was immediately bowled over by the opulence of the ultramodern facility. He had known there was big money in Brunei, but he had not known that the benefits of that prosperity were extended to the masses there. It was patently obvious to him that the dossier compiled for him by his staff had been woefully inadequate, and he resolved to do some research of his own as soon as he was settled in his suite at the Empire Hotel & Country Club in Bandar Seri Begawan.

An unsmiling man in a black chauffeur's livery and bearing a neatly printed cardboard sign with "Duckworth" on it greeted him the instant he exited the jetway and escorted him out to a gleaming black stretch limousine with dark tinted windows. The chauffeur opened the door for him and closed it behind him. Bill set his briefcase on the seat beside him and opened it, beginning to reread the heads of agreement prepared for him by his staff for the joint drilling venture with the government of the Sultanate of Brunei.

He paid little attention to the sights outside the limousine as it entered and emerged from a large traffic circle and turned onto a large modern four-lane highway. He looked up from his documents and noticed a massive stadium off to his right just before the limo entered into another traffic circle and turned onto a much narrower two-lane street. When he glanced back down at the documents, he didn't notice the trees and greenery closing in towards the sides of the roadway.

The limo suddenly screeched to a halt, all four tires locking up. He heard shouting and then saw the limo driver opening the front door and diving out. A split-second later all the rear doors were jerked open and several men armed with AK-47s and dressed all in black swarmed inside the limo and wrestled him to the floorboard. Just before he lost consciousness he realized that the handkerchief they were holding over his nose smelled like chloroform...

A Brad Jacobs Thriller Series by Scott Conrad:

TRACK DOWN AFRICA – BOOK 1

TRACK DOWN ALASKA – BOOK 2

TRACK DOWN AMAZON – BOOK 3

TRACK DOWN IRAQ – BOOK 4

TRACK DOWN BORNEO – BOOK 5

TRACK DOWN EL SALVADOR – BOOK 6

TRACK DOWN WYOMING – BOOK 7

Visit the author at: ScottConradBooks.com

Printed in Great Britain
by Amazon